Selected by *THE NEW YORK TIMES* as one of the
Best Novels published in Latin America in 2017

Selected by *EL PAÍS* as one of the
20 Best Latin American Books of 2017

Selected by *PÁGINA/12* as one of the
Best Latin American books dealing with
feminism, sisterhood and queerness.

Selected by *LOS InROCKUPTIBLES* as one of the
Best Nine Novels published in 2017

THE ADVENTURES OF
CHINA IRON

First published by Charco Press 2019
Charco Press Ltd., Office 59, 44-46 Morningside Road, Edinburgh
EH10 4BF

Copyright © Gabriela Cabezón Cámara 2017
Published by arrangement with Agencia Literaria CBQ SL
First published in Spanish as *Las aventuras de la China Iron* by
Penguin Random House Group (Argentina)
English translation copyright © Iona Macintyre & Fiona Mackintosh 2019

Work published with funding from the 'Sur' Translation Support Programme
of the Ministry of Foreign Affairs of Argentina / Obra editada en el marco
del Programa 'Sur' de Apoyo a las Traducciones del Ministerio de Relaciones
Exteriores de la República Argentina.
World English rights were acquired with funding from the University of
Edinburgh.

A CIP catalogue record for this book is available from the British Library.

ISBN: 978-1-9164656-6-4
e-book: 978-1-9993684-2-5

www.charcopress.com

Edited by Fionn Petch
Cover design by Pablo Font
Typeset by Laura Jones
Proofread by Charlotte Coombe

LOTTERY FUNDED

Gabriela Cabezón Cámara

THE ADVENTURES OF
CHINA IRON

Translated by
Iona Macintyre and Fiona Mackintosh

CHARCO PRESS

Contents

PART ONE: THE PAMPAS

PART TWO: THE FORT

PART THREE: INDIAN TERRITORY

PART ONE

THE PAMPAS

It Was the Brightness of the Light

It was the brightness of the light. The young pup, radiating life, was scampering excitedly between the dusty sore paws of the few dogs left round there. Poverty yields cracked skin. It carves and slowly scrapes away at its young, and leaves them to fend for themselves in all weathers. It makes skin dry, leathery, and scarred, and forces its offspring into unwonted shapes. But not yet the pup: it radiated sheer delight at being alive and gave off a light undimmed by the dingy sadness of a poverty that was, I'm sure, as much a lack of ideas as anything else.

We didn't often go hungry, but everything was grey and dusty, everything was so drab that when I saw the pup I knew in an instant what I wanted for myself: something radiant. It wasn't the first time I'd ever seen a young creature, after all I'd already given birth to two children, and it's not as if the pampa never shone. It became dazzling with the rains, reawakened even as it was flooded. No longer flat, it heaved with grain, tents, Indians on the move, white women escaping from captivity, horses swimming with their gaucho riders still astride, while all around the dorado fish darted like lightning into the depths, into the middle of the bursting river. And in each fragment of that river that was devouring its own banks, a bit of sky was reflected. It didn't seem real to witness such a thing, to see the whole world being dragged along, slowly spiralling, muddy and dizzying, a hundred leagues away to the sea.

First men, dogs, horses and calves fought against the choking and gulping river, against the water's power to kill. Several hours later the struggle was over. The lost herd stretched long and wide, the cattle ran wild like the river, dragged rather than herded, the cows and everything around turning somersaults, hooves up, forwards, down, backwards, like spinning tops, cheek by jowl they hurtled onwards, going in alive and coming out as pounds of rotting flesh. It was a rushing river of cattle falling horizontally; that's how rivers flow where I'm from, with a momentum inseparable from drowning. And so back to the dust with which I began, the dust that dulls everything, and back to the resplendence of the pup that I saw as though I'd never seen one before and as if I'd never seen cows swimming before, nor their shining hides, nor the whole pampa ablaze like a wet stone in the midday sun.

I saw the dog and from then on all I wanted was to find that kind of brightness for myself. So the first thing I did was keep the pup. I named him Estreya (which means Star), and that's still his name, even though I've changed mine since then. Now I'm called China, Josephine Star Iron and Tararira. From the old days I've only kept Iron (the English for Fierro), which was never *my* name to begin with, and Star which I chose when I chose Estreya. My real name? Well, I didn't have one; I was born an orphan, if that's possible, as if the violet-flowered pastures that softened the savagery of the pampa had somehow given birth to me. That's what I used to think whenever I heard the woman who brought me up saying 'it's as if you just sprouted with the weeds'. La Negra: the black woman later widowed by the blade of my brute of a husband's knife. My husband, Martín Fierro, who was probably blind drunk and killed El Negro just for being black, just because he could. Or maybe (and I like imagining this, even of Fierro) he killed him in order to widow La Negra, because she'd treated me like her slave for most of my childhood.

I *was* her slave: a black woman's slave for half my young life and then, very soon after, I was handed over to the gaucho-singer Martín Fierro in holy matrimony. Supposedly El Negro lost me in a drunken game of cards in that dive of a pulpería, and the gaucho-singer wanted me immediately, mere slip of a girl that I was. He wanted to have divine permission, a sacrament so he could throw himself on top of me with God's blessing. And Fierro did throw himself on top of me, by the time I turned fourteen I'd already given him two boys. When they conscripted him and sent him to the Indian frontier (like they conscripted nearly all the men from that poor outpost without even a church to its name) I was left as alone as I must have been the day I was born. A light-haired baby girl in the hands of a black woman, I obviously someone's bastard child.

When they conscripted Fierro along with all the others, they also took Oscar, who was what Fierro laughingly called (in his famous song) a 'Jimmy-gringo' from Britain. The red-head, Elizabeth, whose name I learnt later and would never forget, stayed in the settlement with the intention of getting her husband back. She hadn't been through what I'd been through. I never even considered going after Fierro and certainly not with his two kids in tow. I felt free, as though the ties that bound me were loosening. I left the boys with an old married couple, two farmhands who'd stayed on the estancia. I lied to them and told them I was going to look for Fierro. Back then I didn't care whether their father ever came back. I couldn't have been much older than fourteen years old and I'd had the decency to leave my kids in the care of two kindly old folk who would call them by their names, which is much more than I ever got.

I was tethered by my lack of ideas, by my ignorance. I didn't know I could stand on my own two feet, I didn't realise until I was on my own, unassisted, and was treated a bit like a widow, as if Fierro had died in a heroic act. Even the foreman on the estancia offered me his condolences at the time, my last days as a 'china', as someone's woman. I spent those days feigning pain and suffering, while inside I was so happy that I would run for miles from the settlement to the banks of the brown river, take my clothes off and shout for joy, splashing in the mud with Estreya. I should probably have suspected, but it wasn't until much later that I found out that the list of gaucho conscripts had been drawn up by the self-same foreman who had sent it to the landowner, who had sent it to the sheriff. Fierro, my coward of a husband and a prize charlatan, never sang about that bit of the story.

Had I known I would have thanked them. But there wasn't time. Really just because of her skin colour – because I hadn't seen many pale-skinned people and I harboured the hope that she'd turn out to be related to me – I climbed up onto Elizabeth's wagon. She must have had the same idea because she let me approach her, me, someone with less manners than a mule, less manners than the pup at my side. She looked at me doubtfully, passed me a cup of hot liquid and said 'tea' in English, assuming, correctly, that I wouldn't know the word. 'Tea' she said to me, and that word – which in Spanish, 'ti', sounds like a gift 'to you', 'for you' – is apparently a daily custom in English, and that's how I learnt my first word in that language which was possibly my mother tongue. And tea is what I'm drinking now, while the world seems beset by darkness and violence, by a furious noise that is in fact just one of the frequent storms that shake this river.

The Wagon

It's difficult to know what you remember, is it what actually happened? Or is it the story that you've told and re-told and polished like a gemstone over the course of years, like something that has lustre but is as lifeless as a stone? If it weren't for my dreams, for the recurring nightmare I have where I'm a grubby barefoot girl again, with nothing to my name but a sweet little puppy and a few ragged clothes; if it weren't for the thump I feel here in my chest, the tightness in my throat on the rare occasions that I go to the city and see a skinny, bedraggled little creature hardly there at all; basically, if it weren't for my dreams and the trembling of my body, I wouldn't know that what I'm telling you is true.

Who knows what storms Elizabeth had weathered. Maybe loneliness. She had two missions in life: to rescue her gringo husband and take charge of the estancia that they were to oversee. It suited her to have someone translate for her, someone not afraid to speak up beside her in the wagon. It was something like that anyway, though I think there was more to it. I remember the look on her face that day; I saw the light in her eyes, she opened the door to the world for me. She was holding the reins and driving without knowing exactly where she was going in that wagon that had in it a bed and sheets and cups and a teapot and cutlery and petticoats and so many things I didn't know about. I stood looking up at her with the same trust with which Estreya looked at me every so often when we walked along the fields together. Field or fields, it was hard to know whether to use the singular or the plural for that endless plain until a bit later when the fences and landowners arrived, that settled it. But not back then, in those days the estancia was just a wide-open space. We'd walk through the countryside and sometimes Estreya and I would look at each other and he trusted me the way animals do. In me Estreya saw safety, a home, the knowledge that he wouldn't be abandoned to the elements. That's how I looked at Liz, like a puppy, with the crazy certainty that if she looked back at me in agreement I would have nothing to fear. And she did. That red-headed woman, that woman who was so pale you could see the blood moving in her veins when something made her happy or made her angry. Later I would see her blood freeze from fear, fizz with desire, and burn with rage.

Estreya leapt up onto the wagon with me, and Elizabeth made room for us on the driver's seat. Day was dawning, light was filtering through the clouds, a soft rain fell, and when the oxen lumbered off, there was a moment that was pale and golden, and tiny droplets of rain sparkled in the breeze, and the grassland was greener than ever. Then it began to pour and everything shone, even the dark grey of the clouds; it was the beginning of another life. It was a radiant omen. Thus bathed, in that luminous body, we set off. 'England', she said. And at that time, for me, that light was called 'light' in English and it was England.

We Come from Dust

We were caressed by that golden light during our first hours together. Una very good sign, she said, and I understood. I don't know how I almost always understood almost everything she said, and I answered her in Spanish saying yes, it has to be a good augury, a buen augurio. And each of us repeated the other's phrase until we could say it properly. We were a chorus in different languages, languages that were the same and different, just like what we said, the same and yet unfathomable until we said them together. We parroted back and forth in our own way, each repeating what the other said until nothing was left of the words but the sound, good sign, buen augurio, good augurio, buen sign, guen signurio, guen signurio, guen signurio. We always ended up laughing, and then what we said seemed like chanting that would end up who knows where: the pampa is also a world fashioned so that sound can travel in all directions, little more than silence reigns there. The wind, the call of a chimango bird, the insects when they get very close to your face and — almost every night except the rawest winter's night — the sound of the crickets.

The three of us set off. I didn't feel as though I was leaving anything behind, just the dust raised by the wagon which that morning wasn't much; we drove along an old

Indian trail, one of those tracks the Indians had made when they were able to come and go freely, leaving the earth so firm underfoot that the ground was still well trodden all those years later. I wasn't sure how many, just that it was more than I'd been alive for.

Soon enough the sun lost its golden sheen, it stopped caressing us, and it began to stick to our skin. Figures were still casting a shadow almost all the time but the midday sun was starting to burn. It was September and the earth was breaking open with the tender green of new shoots. She put on a hat and put one on me and so it was that I learnt what life outdoors could be like without blistered skin. Then came the dust: the wind carried the dust raised by the wagon, and all the dust from the land around, straight at us; it covered our faces, our clothes, the animals, the whole wagon. I quickly understood that we had to keep the canvas closed and keep the inside free from dust, that this was what mattered most to my friend. This was one of my greatest challenges during the whole journey. We spent entire days wiping everything; we had to fight to save every single object from the dust. Liz lived in fear of being swallowed whole by that savage land. She was scared we'd all be gobbled up, that we'd end up being a part of it like Jonah became part of the whale. I learned that the whale was similar to a fish. A bit like a dorado fish from the river but grey, with a huge head, the size of a wagon train and likewise able to carry things inside itself, that whale of God had transported a prophet and furrowed the sea the way we furrowed the land. The whale sang a song in her deep voice about water and wind, she danced, she leapt and she squirted water through a hole on the top of her head. Up there driving the wagon, free and whale-like between heaven and earth, I swam.

The first price we had to pay for such happiness was

the dust. I, having lived wholly inside the dust, having been little more than one of the many forms that dust took there, having been contained in that atmosphere – the earth of the pampa is also sky – started to feel it, to notice it, to hate it when it made my teeth gritty, when it stuck to my sweat, when it weighed down my hat. We declared war on the dust, all the while knowing that we were fighting a losing battle: we come from dust.

But ours was a day-to-day war, it wouldn't be forever.

La China Isn't a Name

As soon as we came to a riverbank, the Gringa brought the oxen, horses and wagon to a halt and smiled at us both. Estreya scampered round her, wagging his whole body, dancing for sheer joy and delight. Elizabeth smiled at us as she went into the wagon. I was still waiting for her permission to be allowed in, but she didn't let me, she came straight out again with soap and a brush, and still smiling and making friendly gestures, she took my scrappy clothes off as well as her own, grabbed Estreya and plunged us both into the river, which wasn't as muddy brown as the one other river I knew. She washed herself, her fair freckly skin, ginger pubis, pink nipples, she looked like a heron, a ghost made flesh. She rubbed my head with soap, making my eyes sting. I laughed, we both did. I gave Estreya a good wash too, and once we were clean we carried on splashing about in the water. Liz got out first, wrapped me in a white towel, brushed my hair, put me in a petticoat and dress and then, when that was all done, she came back with a mirror, and there I was inside. I'd never seen myself except reflected in the mostly calm water of the lake, where my reflection was crisscrossed with fish, reeds and crabs. I saw myself looking like her, a señorita, little lady, Liz said, and I started behaving like one, and although I never rode side-saddle and soon would be using the baggy gaucho trousers the Gringo had left in the wagon, that day I became a lady for ever, even when riding bareback like an Indian and slitting a cow's throat with one slash of a gaucho knife.

We also sorted out the issue of names – it was an afternoon for baptising things. 'Me Elizabeth', she kept repeating and eventually I learnt to say it: Elizabeth, Liz, Ellie, Elizabeta, Elisa. 'Liz', she said firmly, and that's how it was. 'What you name?' she asked me in the broken Spanish she spoke back then. 'La China', I answered. 'That's not a name', Liz said. 'China', I insisted, and I was right, that's what La Negra used to shout at me, La Negra who would later be widowed by my good-for-nothing husband. China is what he'd call me last thing at night as he dropped off to sleep, 'safe and sound in the arms of love' as he put it later in one of his songs. He also shouted China when he wanted his food or his trousers or mate to drink or anything else. I was La China. Liz told me that where I was from, all women were called chinas but they each had their own name as well. Not me. At that point I didn't understand why she got so upset, why her little pale blue eyes started to fill up. 'We can do something about that', she said – I don't know which language she said it in, nor how I understood her – and she started pacing up and down with Estreya jumping at her feet. 'How would you like to be called Josefina?' she said, turning to look directly at me. I liked the name: La China Josefina couldn't be keener, La China Josefina's hands are cleaner, La China Josefina's figure is leaner, La China Josefina has a serene demeanour. La China Josefina was good. China Josephine Iron, she named me, deciding that for want of another surname, I'd better use the one belonging to my no-good husband. I said I'd like to take Estreya's name too, so I'd be China Josephine Star Iron. She kissed me lightly on the cheek, I hugged her, then I set about the none-too-easy task of getting a fire going and cooking some meat without singeing or spoiling my nice dress, which I managed. That night I slept inside the wagon, which was much more of a home than my old shack. The wagon had whisky, a wardrobe, hocks of ham, biscuits, a shelf of books, bacon, oil lamps… Liz taught me the name of each thing. And best of all, at least by the standards of a young woman on her own, two shotguns and three full boxes of gun cartridges.

I hugged Estreya tight as he curled up with Liz, plunging myself into their newly-washed, floral smell. I wrapped myself in those lavender-scented sheets, only later figuring out that the smell wasn't a quality of the cloth the way the texture was, that smoothness which enveloped me that night and all the nights of what would be – broadly speaking and dividing things rather dramatically – the rest of my life. Among those perfumed sheets I felt Liz's breath, smooth and spiced, and I just wanted to stay there, immerse myself in her breath, though I didn't quite know how. I slept, peaceful and happy, snug amongst perfumes, bedclothes, dog hair, red hair and the shotgun.

Everything Covered Me
like a Second Skin

Dear old Estreya, sparky and with a blue sheen to his black fur, was no longer new to the world and was learning nearly as much as me. We were growing up together: when we left, he only came up to my knee, and me, up to Liz's shoulder. When we arrived, and we didn't know we were arriving, he reached my waist and I was nearly as tall as Liz. I remember him as a puppy, sitting up straight like a gentleman with his ears down, eyes intent, and nose wet, even now he's touchingly innocent when he trusts in the results of his good manners. I lived in a similar innocence, though I was beginning to feel a new fear. While I used to be afraid that there was nothing to life but La Negra, Fierro, and our ramshackle hut, now I feared the end of our journey, of the wagon, the smell of lavender, the shape of my first letters, the porcelain, the shoes with heels and laces, and all the words in two languages. I dreaded seeing anger on Liz's face, or glimpsing something undefined and ghostly hiding behind a sand dune – sand dunes were starting to appear – or between the roots of an ombú tree, or out there in the dark amongst the creatures whose noises broke the silence. The creatures of the pampas are nocturnal, they come out of their tunnels and caves as darkness falls. I was afraid that something would send me back to my old hut and to my life as a china.

I had gone from the raw to the cooked: the leather of my new boots was just as much leather as the leather on Fierro's saddle, but it wasn't the same kind of leather. The leather of the shoes Liz gave me was burgundy, glossy and supple, and it fitted my feet like a second skin. It wasn't just the shoes and the leather: it was the cotton sheets, my silk petticoat from China – the real China where the girls really are chinas – the jerseys and the wool: everything covered me like a second skin. Everything was smooth and warm and caressed me and every step filled me with happiness, every morning when I put on my petticoat and the dress and jersey on top, I felt that at last I was complete in the world, as if up till then I'd been naked, flayed even. Only at that point did it hit me. The pain of being left to fend for myself at the mercy of the elements, before being dressed in these fabrics. I felt a violent passion for my clothes, my dog, my friend, a love which was as much fear as happiness, fear that they'd get broken, that I'd lose them, a love which swelled up and made me laugh till I could scarcely breathe, a heart-stopping love which came out in over-protectiveness towards the dog, the woman and my clothes, a love that watched over them with a shotgun. I was as happy as I was unhappy and that was more than I'd ever felt before.

I wore wool a lot because we set off at the beginning of spring and it was still quite cold. I don't think I've mentioned it yet but we were heading towards Indian Territory, to the desert.

Under the British Empire

One rainy dawn I put on my first ever raincoat. 'The subjects of the British Empire have appropriate etiquette for all occasions', Liz explained, outlining their manners and mountain ranges, their climates, deserts and forests. The details of all the clothing in the Empire built the world for me, a world that was round not flat. I'd never thought about it till then, my world map hardly stretched beyond the pampas and a few vague notions: Indian Territory, Buenos Aires, a watery abyss and then Europe, with Spain at the bottom and up there the British Isles, the cradle of men and weapons. This ball-shaped world came to life through Liz's stories, half in Spanish, half in English. She started populating it with sacred cows, soft saris, hot Indian curry, African tribesmen with painted faces, elephants with tusks the length of a small tree, huge eggs laid by ostriches, the larger cousins of our ñandús, Chinese paddy fields, curly-roofed pagodas and coolie hats pointing up to the sky. As we travelled I began to understand some of these things, but the rest I understood much later, over the course of all the time we spent together. I found it hard to reconcile myself to the idea that we were on the bottom half of a globe when we seemed to be on the top, but no, Liz was sure that Great Britain was on top. How could that be? It was quite plain that your feet were on the ground wherever you were, even in the land of pygmies, gorillas and diamonds (hard transparent stones that are wrenched from deep inside rocks). She insisted that on top was Great Britain, the land where machines moved by themselves with burning wood as though movement was a huge bonfire, or as if the pieces of burning wood were horses. Or oxen, like ours, the four strong, docile oxen who pulled the wagon which enfolded me just like the silk petticoat and the awning proofed with wax that at the end of the day was just tallow from a cow, though it had previously been filtered many times through sandalwood and smelled like a heady flower, like a laudanum flower, I mean, like a drug, just like opium must smell. Opium was like caña but much stronger than our drink, she explained to me, and so many people succumbed to it in the North African heat, where men swathe their heads in a few metres of cloth for a hat, and women are covered from head to toe. The raincoat with its eastern smells covered me. The wagon, waxed like the raincoat and smelling the same, covered us. All three of us – not just me, but Estreya, who travelled on Liz's lap to begin with, while I took the reins, and Liz herself. It was like we were secreting fine threads to make a shell or carapace, woven together like a kind of house made not from spider's silk, straw, mud or the leathery shell of a crab, but gradually formed from the loops of words and gestures. From Liz's story and my care for each of our possessions, a space was emerging. One that was ours, with the wagon which went steadily forward, with that empty land which was becoming as flat as it seems to those who have known hills and mountains. The vastness of the pampas was becoming flatter to me with every new tale of bustling London's smoky sprawl; the desert horizon widened against a backdrop of African jungles; the prickly grass, the waving grass and the scrubby bushes became squat in contrast to the forests of Europe; these rivers without banks paled against her English rivers flanked by red-brick houses, so very different to our rivers bordered by mud and with nothing around but reeds, rushes, herons and flamingos, Liz's favourites – luckily she likes the strong colours of the pampas. She said that everything there was shades of brown against the endlessly pale and transparent blue of the sky, except when the dust rose, or when different hues of green appeared, the young wheat springing green and glorious after summer rain, only matched, we thought then, by the green and pleasant fields of England.

You only get the other colours in the sky at dawn or dusk, or in the flamingos who are always colourful. It was raining again and light was reflected on all living things, and on the dead, just the odd cow bone at that stage. The earth was burnished copper and our protective shell was growing around us, keeping the three of us warm. We were sustained by Liz's words, Estreya's pink tongue, and my rapture at being there, calm as a well-fed animal in the sun.

Calm, but slightly confused: according to Liz, the earth was a round ball, and we were at the bottom. Maybe there was something about a stone in the North that pulled everything towards it, above Great Britain, because there was something above England, above everything, Liz explained, where the planet's hat would be if the planet was a head, a head without a neck. What, with its head chopped off? No, just a round head without a body. Just a head, did I understand? No I didn't; I'd never seen a head without a body. No, of course not, it was just an example. An example, she explained to me, was something you said to make an idea clear. But you don't get heads without bodies, I insisted, so what can it be an example of, if it doesn't exist? An example of things that don't exist, but you're right, she said, and she went back to talking about the planet, and this time she used the example of a little orange, which made it much easier for me to imagine: it clearly has a top, where the stalk connects it to the tree, and a bottom. And which tree does the earth hang from? It doesn't. So the orange didn't help me much either. Anyhow, I began thinking that on the top half of the planet, not just in England, things grew upwards more easily. Apparently there were hills and mountains and it was full of tall trees as high as several men on top of each other. How many men? The highest trees would be ten or fifteen men high. Do they look like ombús? A bit, but the trees there are taller than they are wide, elongated; the ombú is squat, as if gravity was stronger in the bottom half of the planet and everything was flattened or forced underground. Gravity was what made things fall down. So how come it didn't squash us all – me, Liz, Estreya, the wagon, the oxen, mules, cows and horses?

That night, Liz made a stew out of an armadillo that I'd caught and butchered. She cooked the poor creature in its own shell. She added ingredients that I was beginning to recognise; a mixture of onion, garlic and ginger with cloves, cinnamon, cardamom, chilli pepper, peppercorns, cumin and mustard seeds. Everything bubbled away in the shell, and when it was done, Estreya and I had our first taste of spicy food. Everything we were experiencing was new to us; ideas, sensations and even our taste buds were expanding under the British Empire.

Dragons and My Pampa

All Mixed Up Together

While the land grew into a whole globe in front of me, another world took shape on the wagon. Me, Liz and Estreya were a trinity, within a rectangle starting from the oxen, one line along the roof, another at the trunk to the rear of the wagon and one running along the ground.

'Only here in the pampa could a wagon create a bird's-eye view', observed Liz and so I found out what perspective was and noted that indeed, the few animals that stand out on the plains – hares, cuys and armadillos, the flamingos in the lagoons, herons, the occasional puma if we managed to see one – are always alert and quick but they take fright at just about everything. Anyway, the fauna of the flat pampas seemed to be stuck to the ground. The animals didn't stretch up like giraffes, those amiable-looking, long-necked animals that eat from the tops of trees; nor did they extend themselves like gigantic elephants, using their trunks like hands. From up high or from down low the world looked different; it also looked different from behind a turning wagon wheel or from the highest branches of an ombú. In those days of discovery I tried looking from lots of different angles: I walked on all fours seeing what Estreya saw, the pasture, the creepy crawlies that went about on the surface of the earth, cows' udders, Liz's hands, her face, food on plates, and everything that moved. I leant my head on the heads of the oxen and I put my hands next to my eyes and I saw what they saw, only what was right in front of them, the cattle track and the uncertain horizon they strove to reach. I also stood on my hands, seeing first feet and knees and wheels and hooves and then what was above them. And I began to see other perspectives: the Queen of England – a rich, powerful woman who owned millions of people's lives, but who was sick and tired of jewels and of meals in palaces built where she was monarch of all she surveyed – didn't see the world in the same way as, for example, a gaucho in his hovel with his leather hides who burns dung to keep warm. For the Queen, the world was a sphere filled with riches belonging to her, and that she could order to be extracted from anywhere; for the gaucho, the world was a flat surface where you galloped about rounding up cows, cutting the throats of your enemies before they cut your own throat, or fleeing conscription and battles. I took over the cooking some nights so that Liz could draw all the things I couldn't quite imagine from her descriptions: I had my special loves. I loved the tiger, like a giant orange stripy puma, I loved the hippopotamus, an animal with an enormous mouth and the square teeth of a child, a kind of wagon with hard skin and four fat short legs, a creature that likes to live inside rivers, and I loved zebras, those African horses with stripes. But the dragon aroused such passion in me, that beautiful beast made from horrible beasts: the eyes of a locust, the horns of a zebu, the snout of an ox, the nose of a dog, the whiskers of a catfish, the shaggy mane of a ñandú, the tail of a viper, the scales of a fish, the claws of a gigantic chimango, and with potent phlegm made of fire. The dragon was an animal that I liked to imagine flying above our heads and over our roof like a guardian angel: why shouldn't a wagon be a house protected by a dragon? Liz liked to captivate me, she needed my awe-struck gaze, my laughter, the joy that her tales and her exquisite drawings, so beautifully precise, gave me. This I understood when I saw myself drawn by her, looking just like what I saw every morning in the looking glass, but made of lines, without colour. She told me the story of the dragon one night, while I was grilling some tararira fish I had just caught. About how the first four dragons had been born in the China Sea, and how they played around flying and swimming and breathing fire all the time; about how one day they felt sorry that men were going hungry, and about how they flew to see the Emperor of the Sky who was listening to a fairy orchestra in his jade palace. About how he turned to them, furious at having been interrupted, and although he promised rain, the rain never came; about how the four dragons then decided to take water to spit on the earth, about how the emperor got angry, about how he buried them under rocks as enormous as everything we could see as far as the horizon; about how the dragons cried and cried until they turned to water and formed the four rivers of China that were called the Long River, the Yellow River, the Black River and the Pearl River, because those were the dragon's names.

I slept like a baby once Liz had explained to me what jade, fairies and an emperor were, and what the fire was that came out of the insides of those good animals who were turned to water. I put the shotgun away, dragons and my pampa all mixed up together, all the while asking myself if it was thanks to the dragons that the whole earth shone when the river burst its banks.

At the Mercy of the Caranchos

It only took a few days of wagon, dust and stories for us to become a family. Entwined in our burgeoning love we laughed at old fears of being abandoned, of being defeated, of falling to the ground without the strength to get up, stuck to the ground and left at the mercy of the caranchos, of being reduced to what we are: a structure of bones and minerals, like stones. Weaving ourselves as one, we were slow to notice that the near nothingness we were crossing was starting to look like an abandoned burial ground; we ploughed on blithely, as if we were travelling through paradise, though maybe I'm wrong, maybe paradise isn't a place to travel through, it's simply a place to be. Where would one want to go from here?

Days of going more or less in a straight line had passed without us seeing a single cow, Indian, white man, or horse. Weeks of flat days as if there was nothing in the world but weeds, one or two little mules, and the caranchos. Occasionally at night a hare would be dazzled by the light from our campfire and Estreya would give chase and sometimes catch it. That and the earth pearled with bones when the wind or rain came. The dust was merciful, covering everything including the skeletons lying by the wayside; little by little it covered them leaving faint relief carvings, imperceptible burial mounds, little more than oversized ant hills, but also teeming with life, the life of worms born in dead flesh.

Until the rain came again and once more we'd see a cemetery of Indian braves at our feet: we could make them out because they were one with their weapons and animals, as if the heroic skeletons of the pampas were centaur fossils, said Liz. I didn't know what a centaur was and I definitely didn't know that Indians could be brave. I think it was with that story and that discussion that we reached the third week of our journey. We rested, we washed again, this time in an almost crystalline river with just a pair of herons for company. Nor did I know what a desert was, even though I realised that so much emptiness couldn't have been the natural state of this pampa. I didn't know that a desert was exactly that, a territory with no population, no trees, no birds, without almost any sign of life in the day except for us. I thought desert was the name of the place where nobody lived but Indians. Either way, the desert was getting more and more frightening; we started having nightmares, sometimes even in the daytime. I began writing in order to fend off these nightmares. Liz would teach me my letters and tell me what prayer to say at bedtime. I still know some. 'Dear Lord, please send us un amigo. And save us from the quagholes'.

And if trust in our prayers wasn't enough to send us off to sleep, Liz and I would drink a whisky, that elixir of life in Britain, water from Scotland's water and above all, she explained to me, earth from Scotland's earth, which turned barley into this nectar. They soaked the grain in hot water and left it till it sprouted. Then they dried it using a smoke made with tree branches, with sticks and sometimes with peat, a kind of earth made of plants that haven't become earth yet. We could make whisky. We really could: we just had to get some grain, some oak barrels and funnels, some stills with long iron tubes. The snag is how long you have to wait: it takes whisky twelve years in the barrels before it's ready. I liked whisky and I also liked the fact that I liked it: I wanted to be British too.

Lost in Thought, into the Muck I Sank

I told Liz, redheaded Liz – my new friend, my first ever – about it all, about the second beginning of my life, the only beginning that matters to me. The other one I don't remember, but if I do, I forget all about it again thanks to the whisky, my new languages, the river, the voices from my house, my dog, the rain and the bees. The river devoured that past but a quaghole could have swallowed it whole. I'd heard of wagons, armies, mules, cities made of stone, silver and gold, Spanish galleons full of men armed with arquebuses, I'd heard of so many things that the mud could swallow. That's why the Indians walked so lightly and didn't dare put anything other than tents on the ground and didn't use furniture other than sheep-skins and animal hides, or so I thought. Anyway, we had to follow the Indian trail, so sure was Liz that her estancia lay in the direction of the Indian hordes. Inside her wagon, already *our* wagon by then, she had a compass and a great big map all folded up on itself: it showed the continents, seas, rivers, the mountains in brown, and the plains like my pampa in green. Not a single route marked in the direction we were heading. That was what the compass was for, to know where the North is, that icy land, the hat on top of the planet, pulling like a magnet, which is a piece of metal that attracts other pieces so much that they stick together. Not long after that, during our long spell in the desert, I learned it was called a brújula in my language. We're like the children of Israel, Liz would say, but instead of raining down manna on us, every so often God makes cuys and armadillos appear from under our feet. They did spring from the ground, she was right, not thanks to any miracle, but because I smoked them out of their burrows. After giving them a sharp whack with a stick, and without looking into their little eyes, so like ours, I dispatched the poor things straight onto the grill. Having just found out about the spherical nature of the world, I reckoned the animals must come out of the ground because in the South, Jehovah sends us food from below, rather than making it fall from the heavens via miracles and gravity. If you really think about it, it's even more miraculous the way our food pops out of the earth and offers itself to us, defying gravity. Though, to be fair, it didn't actually offer itself to us. They kicked, squealed, and bit us, the little varmints, never giving themselves up or giving in.

I felt I'd lived outside everything, outside of the world that fitted snugly into the wagon along with Estreya and Liz, a world that was already becoming second nature. I learnt what a compass was, the same way I learnt to wear a petticoat and write the alphabet. A bit like learning to swim, that was my new life: thrown into deep water. Our journey too was something like sailing, following in the wake of the Indians, the same route along which the military forts had been built. Oscar the Gringo would be in one of them. So would Fierro, but whatever it took I was planning to stay in the world of the compass, which was his world, Liz's husband's I mean, who'd been a sailor. So was Liz in a way. Following the path of the Indian hordes, I began avoiding the quagholes like someone avoiding rocks at sea. We learnt how to find out if the Indians were close by examining the dung left by their animals. It was always dry until one fateful day, when what we wanted – and feared – happened: I stepped in a huge pile of steaming dung in my little Victorian lace-up boots and, lost in thought, into the muck I sank.

When I wasn't chatting to Liz or playing with Estreya I was always lost in thought, living in a daydream. Up until that point my life had been absent somehow. My life hadn't been my own, maybe that was why I was always so far away, maybe not, I don't know. The damp smelly dung jolted me out of it. The Indians were near. Or a couple of their animals had run away. We didn't know. I got into the wagon. I took off my dress and the petticoats and I put on the Englishman's breeches and shirt. I put on his neckerchief and asked Liz to take the scissors and cut my hair short. My plait fell to the ground and there I was, a young lad. Good boy she said to me, then pulled my face towards her and kissed me on the mouth. It surprised me, I didn't under-stand, I didn't know you could do that and it was revealed to me so naturally: why wouldn't you be able to do that? It's just that back where I came from women didn't kiss each other, though I did remember cows sometimes mounting other cows. I liked it, Liz's imperious tongue entered my mouth, her spicy, flowery saliva tasted like curry and tea and lavender water. I would have liked it to go on longer, but when I grabbed her tight by the hair and pressed my tongue between her teeth she pushed me away.

I wasn't sure if that kiss was a British custom or an inter-national sin. I didn't care, Liz loved me, that much was clear, and even if it wasn't, there was no going back. From then on, I kept watch, I was always on my horse and stuck close to Estreya, who was also transformed. He went on the alert, becoming a guard dog in the blink of an eye, just like I'd become a boy with a shotgun. Suddenly there was a clap of thunder and I dashed into Liz's bed for the rest of the watch.

The Morbid Light of Dead Men's Bones

It poured with rain and the water swept away the merciful dust: all was mud and protruding bones. White bones, pearly and iridescent like a devil's lantern, the morbid light of dead men's bones, of mortal remains, of skeletons. Bad sign, said Liz, and I was inclined to agree. Those white bones tinged with a bluish gleam by flashes of lightning were the bones of men and women. Some were already bleached and bare as if scrubbed and polished by an army of skilled craftsmen. Others were not, and they slowly decomposed like little suppurating mounds. My Englishwoman was indignant: Savages! They should bury them. Only animals leave dead bodies lying about. She was right, only savages leave the dead unburied, to be picked at by chimangos. My people were savages, and the pampas a sickening dung heap of Indians and white men.

Tank You Señora for Cure Me

The rain stopped and we had two or three days of flat horizon, and of being pulled between the fear of being seen and the hope that we would meet others along the way. Until suddenly, against that endless backdrop of the horizon, the earth rose up like tempestuous waves in a storm. We weren't thrown off, but I reined in hard and the sudden standstill nearly caused the wagon to spew out the half of England we were carrying. Our bodies bore the brunt, as our belongings struck us, not that we felt it, so horror-struck were we by the sight of the pampa erupting. The earth shook itself up, sweeping skywards in spirals that merged and thrust themselves towards the wagon, blinding us. The three of us and our oxen and horses stayed so still that within seconds it had engulfed us like a solid mass of dust, punctured by the unearthly cries of the few birds that live in the pampas and by Estreya barking at the brown cloud from under the feet of the oxen, who were frozen to the spot. Then, as if the birds were lightning and cattle thunder, we heard the low rumble of a stampeding herd. We shook, everything shook, and everything that had fallen on us started shifting, covering us again until the noise became deafening. Then just like that it stopped: no more clamour of hooves, barking or birdcalls. We couldn't hear anything, couldn't see anything; the earth had swallowed us up. We were as still as Lot's wife, but so drenched in sweat that we were turned to mud. We smelled dung and could hear what seemed like the world itself gasping for breath until the dust settled and we saw that we were surrounded by about a thousand head of cattle. They were the same brown as everything else at that point, long eyelashes fluttering and tails flicking with either fear or affection. The cows and bulls encircled us, calm now as if they'd just come home, as if they'd found shelter around our wagon, as if the mere fact of protecting us, Estreya, the oxen, my little horse and the wagon somehow protected them too. Nothing moved, just the dust falling in a gentle haze, and us stock-still amidst this slow revelation of dark animal hides and the dust smudging the air as it fell.

At some point the calm was broken: the herd parted like a brown sea to let through a man on horseback, carrying a lamb on the saddle. He bid us good day and said how pleased he was to meet some folks at last. He was on his way to Indian Territory looking for a place to set up with his cattle, and where were we headed? Liz said we were going the same way, Indian Territory. He chuckled and we saw that he had a kind, childish face; this man in front of us looked like a little orphan, but no, at that point at least, he wasn't the orphan. Stroking the baby lamb, he explained that he'd taken it in because its mother had died. He seemed happy to meet an Englishwoman and a blond boy in the middle of nowhere, he talked non-stop and tried to make Liz talk so he could laugh at her every word. She had to explain England to him, the ocean, the steamer, the desire to travel to the other side of the world. What on earth for? For the same reason as you, Liz replied, to find somewhere to live with my cattle. And where are your cattle, señora? The gaucho's eyes lit up with amusement when Liz explained to him that some of her cows were coming across, as she had done, on a boat. But why, when we've got plenty here already? To improve the stock, of course, since British cows were superior, like almost everything else from Britain. Liz didn't actually say that last bit, as she started explaining that it was the breeds from Scotland, where she came from, that were the very best. So then she had to explain Scotland, even though she'd never get the Argentines to stop calling her English. I think Rosario, that was the gaucho's name, started getting bored with so many explanations, because he interrupted Liz and said he felt like throwing some beef on the fire, if we were interested. We were, Liz always loved asado, so she accepted heartily saying we had firewood and that someone would have to milk the cows. Jo, would you do it?

I went and milked one of the runaways, who was quite docile about it and seemed relieved. I knew a fair bit about cows, although I'd never really stopped to look at their faces. The runaway and I looked at each other, she batted her eyelashes in what I took to be gratitude, as if the milk had been weighing her down. I kept looking and saw in her round, untroubled eyes, her good cow eyes, an abyss, a deep longing for pasture, for a track, for fields of sunflowers even. All this I seemed to glimpse in her pupils along with her urge to lick her calf. She began licking the calf there and then and I looked down and got on with my milking and decided to give her a name, I called her Curry. When I'd finished, both the calf and Estreya started suckling. Estreya had hardly ever had milk in his life and he went at it delightedly until he was sated and lay on his back with his paws curled up, his tail waggling on the ground in ecstasy.

Rosario the gaucho introduced himself again while he laid the fire and prepared a spit for cooking the beef, he paused briefly to tear off a piece of the animal's stomach lining that was a bit dry but still flexible, and he filled it with the milk I gave him and fed the lamb, who then went to sleep at his feet by the fireside. 'The lamb's called Braulio. He's male,' Rosario pointed out.

That it was male was obvious. I was the one Rosario was probably confused about, with my men's clothes and my smooth cheeks. And Liz calling me 'Jo'. I didn't offer any explanation, I just helped him gather firewood and stroked the lamb while Estreya sniffed at it in wonder. The way the gaucho had nursed the little lamb was so touching. Yet when he'd built the fire, he stood up, unsheathed his knife, grabbed a calf, stunned it with a stone to the head and slit its throat. Its mother's distressed moaning made us all feel awful. Rosario surprised me once again with his tenderness: after having killed the calf he went up to the cow and stroked it, asking her forgiveness and feeding her some grass from his hand. The cow carried on lowing dolefully and stumbling around, butting other calves with her head. She was looking for her own calf, which by now was splayed over the fire. I thought for a moment about my little ones, my little boys, but barely, I couldn't afford to think too much, or cry or let anything drag me back to my life in the shack: I was leaving that behind.

So now we were four with Rosario, Estreya, me and my Liz, as I'd started calling her. Rosario carried on with his asados, his feeding bottles made of tripe, and his little orphans: as well as Braulio, he soon adopted a hare, a cuy and a young foal. They all walked along behind the gaucho as if he was a mother duck and they were his ducklings. At night, before spreading out his poncho if he was sober enough − or collapsing wherever if he wasn't − he would tell us scraps of his life which we'd already half-guessed, having seen how he was. His father died young, his mother was left alone with eight mouths to feed, his stepfather was as vicious as a puma among hens and Rosario, old beyond his years, was forced to flee that cruel life aged ten, pushed to the door by the tip of his stepfather's knife, to nurse his wounds elsewhere. With a limp, and grey before his time, the poor lad was still looking for someone to look after him in that vast nothingness: so we took him in. He stayed with us, looked after us and we looked after him. He laughed at my men's clothing but he understood, he said that he thought it was a good thing me dressing like a man, it was like carrying a knife, all women should carry them the way all men do. We knew he was talking about his mother and how he'd have preferred her to have grown a beard if it meant she'd have stayed a widow with him by her side instead of that monster. After another caña, Rosario demanded more English to make him laugh and Elisa, Elizabeth, sang him her songs or told him stories, and he laughed as if 'two monkeys were dancing minuets upside down'. Then he'd wake up rough, hungover as Liz put it, so she'd lace his mate with whisky and Rosario would come back to life and thank her in the same faltering English every day: 'Tank you señora for cure me.'

By Dint of Force

Liz carried on with her stories about Great Britain. When she went to London, the sky was leaden and smoky from the locomotives and factories, and the almost incessant rain had a sharp tang to it. The air she breathed was damp and grey, with a strange orangey tint, and so heavy and thick that she could almost see it. Yet as soon as she left the city behind, the light gleamed on unbroken fields of grass that stretched all the way to cliffs pounded by the sea. The land ends abruptly there, as if England had been cut off from the rest of the world with an axe, as if the land had been forcibly condemned to an insularity which those of us who live there, we, the British, darling, try to overcome by dint of force, making ourselves the centre, organising the world around us, being the motor, market and matrix of all nations. Here in Argentina we're so far removed from that other island which rises up sustained by its weaponry, its steamships, its machines invented to dominate the world with ever faster production. That island where metal goods reign as intractably as the railroads laid down all over by royal decree so that the fruits of men's labour migrates from fields, mountains and jungles to ports, ships and finally into her own port, to the all-devouring mouth of Kronos. That mouth where everything becomes fuel for its own insatiable speed: from the still-warm hairs on a cowhide to the frozen facets of diamonds, from stretchy rubber to crumbling coal. The power of Great Britain isn't in armies or banks: our strength comes from speed, beating the clock, trailblazing, cutting production times, faster ships, machine guns, banking transactions made in a matter of days, above all the power of the railways dividing the earth, heading for every port laden with imperial manufacturing and returning with spoils and fruits from every land.

Everything was still possible in that languid time of the pampas, during our chats over Rosario's asados. He was constantly amused at the sound of English; 'what's your word for that, señora?' he'd ask Liz, and explode with laughter whenever she answered 'cow', 'sky', 'horse', 'fire' or 'Indians', scattering the birds who were picking ticks off the runaway cows. He would merrily gnaw at a rack of ribs and – in gaucho fashion – wash it all down with caña. Then over pudding he'd start talking to his horses. He was sorry, he said, but the horses couldn't go travelling with Liz because where she came from, wagons moved by themselves. 'Wheels move with rods over there, you poor horses would be out of a job! You'd be up shit creek! You'll just have to stay here with me; where the Gringa comes from, they don't need the likes of you,' and he'd pat them fondly. We laughed too and Estreya ate out of his hand and curled up in Rosario's lap as if he was still just a puppy. Liz sent Rosario off to bed and he did as any gaucho would: he took his poncho and the sheepskin off his saddle and lay down with the animals. He'd taken a shine to Estreya and together they slept out under the stars with Braulio.

We went, just the two of us, into the warm, yellowish fug of the wagon. Liz snuffed out the candles, stripped me of the Gringo's clothes, wiped me down with a damp sponge, dried me, put a petticoat on me, lay down in my arms and went to sleep, as if she hadn't noticed the goose bumps all down my body, nor caught the urgent smell of desire that hung in droplets from the hairs of my pubis until they spread slowly and languorously down my thighs.

That's Also Something You Eat and Drink with Scones

The desert framed the scene, a brownish plain, the same in all directions, a flat surface on which the sky balanced like there was nothing else in the world. You might say that being there, on the wagon box or riding my horse, was living the life of a bird, a bit like flying, your whole body submerged in the air. It doesn't seem right, there are hardly any birds in the pampas and the few we have are low-flying or can't fly at all. You get flamingos like clouds of shrill pink on the horizon. You get ñandús that run faster than horses, their strong elastic legs scything the ground and raising the dust. The ñandús connect pampa and sky. And, like at sea, where you know you're approaching dry land because you start seeing birds overhead, the same happens in the desert with water and groups of people: birds also circle villages and encampments. So being in the pampa was like soaring over a scene with no adventures but its own, its shifting skies and our journeying. Over the dark line of the horizon the sun and the air ravel and unravel. When it's clear, the sun and air are scattered through a prism at different times of day, cut at dawn into reds, purples, oranges and yellows that turn gold as they hit the ground, where the little green takes on a tender and brilliant texture and everything upright casts long soft shadows. Then the sun crushes it all until the prism comes back. And the night in summertime is dark purple and shot through with stars. All that time I had the soles of my feet and my shadow on the ground and the rest of my body up in the sky. You might say that's the same everywhere. But no, back there in my pampa, life is life in the air. Even celestial, sometimes; far from the shack that had been my home, the world was paradise. I can't remember having experienced that before, that total immersion in the endlessly shifting light. I felt the light inside me, felt I was little more than a restless mass of flashes and sparks. Quite possibly I was right about that.

There wasn't much shade for me beyond the sweet-smelling wagon, the only space that seemed more a part of the earth than the sky even though it was a good few feet above the ground. Home always seems fixed to the ground, even when home is a boat. Or a wagon. And that was my first island, the island that took shape for me as we made our journey, a rectangle of wood and canvas that we kept dark and cool to discourage the flies that seemed to come from nowhere and multiply effortlessly. Of course there were carcasses around and we added even more bones to the world every time we slaughtered one of the hundreds of cows following us. We didn't kill many: they're big animals and once we'd butchered one we would cure it making a delicious jerky that Liz had perfected. First she'd plunge the fillets into salt and then steep them in curry and honey. When she reckoned they were ready she'd put them on the fire for a while: they crunched in your mouth, melted salty-sweet and spicy on your tongue, then burned down to your stomach. We didn't even do that at the settlement. We would slaughter a whole cow, eat what was necessary, and then the rest was for the caranchos. Fierro used to say that the caranchos had to eat too, and I tend to think he was right about that, although he didn't take into consideration the huge number of carcasses that our country produced, and not just dead cows; Indian and gaucho corpses also fed several generations of scavenger birds. But going back to my life in the air and my home in the bobbing wagon, like I said, we kept it dark and fresh, and as full of nice smells as an East India Company warehouse. The smell of near-black tea leaves torn from the green mountains of India that would travel to Britain without losing their moisture, and without losing the sharp perfume born of the tears Buddha shed for the world's suffering, suffering that also travels in tea: we drink green mountains and rain, and we also drink what the Queen drinks. We drink the Queen, we drink work, and we drink the broken back of the man bent double as he cuts the leaves, and the broken back of the man carrying them. Thanks to steam power, we no longer drink the lash of the whip on the oarsmen's backs. But we do drink choking coal miners. And that's the way of the world: everything alive lives off the death of someone or something else. Because nothing comes from nothing, Liz explained that to me: everything comes from work; that's also something you eat and drink with scones. Liz would sometimes bake scones in the ovens that I made by digging a pit in the earth. The harder you work, the better it tastes, she declared. I said yes to her, over those months we spent together in the enormous sky of the pampa, I always agreed with her. I could have contradicted her quite easily just by pointing out her delight at asado, something that doesn't really take a lot of work. I didn't though, I didn't contradict her. Back then I thought about it and thought I was being clever. At some point, and I hadn't even said anything – that was how transparent the distance was between us – she answered that asado doesn't require much human effort, but you did need an animal to suffer. She said that even Christ, Our Lord, was made flesh in order to be sacrificed: he had worked for the eternal salvation of all of us, and there has never been a world or a life that wasn't both fuel and flame. And there never would be.

During that entire first journey I didn't argue about anything: I was simply astonished by everything, or did my best to appear astonished, even on the few occasions when I wasn't. It was the first journey; I knew full well that all journeys come to an end, and maybe this experience of time as finite is what lends light and texture to every living moment, knowing that you have to go back home, that you're in a foreign land. I watched hungrily, I collected images, I tried to be alert to everything. I felt things acutely; my whole body, my whole skin was completely alive as if it was made of hunting animals, of felines, of the pumas that we were afraid to meet in the desert. I was awake and aware that life has a perimeter, almost as if I could see it. And in some ways I could: I didn't think too much about death back then, even though we were furrowing a land that seemed to flower with bones every time it rained, but I still felt my body was dirty from my life before Estreya, Liz and the wagon. Just putting one of my feet down on the ground was enough for me to be overcome by the smell of wet earth, I was deafened by the scuffling of the cuys, every gust of wind made me shiver, I was caressed by the fragrance of the mint that grew among the weeds and of the small orange and purple flowers strung together in the mud, and I was stung by the prickly thistles. Liz's cooking made my mouth water – she artfully managed to make hearty breakfasts in the ovens dug out of the earth: scrambled eggs, bacon, toast, orange juice till the oranges ran out, tea, fried tomatoes, beans. And Liz's body held me like the sun does a sunflower, I would have found it hard to keep my head upright on my shoulders if she had stopped looking at me. I felt the force of this attraction like a gravitational pull, that force that allows us to stand. She was my North and I was the quivering needle on a compass: my whole body was pulled towards her, dwarfed by the strength of my desires. It was under the sway of that force that I began to feel, and now I think perhaps it's always that way, that you feel the world through others, through your bonds with others. I felt alive, as fierce as a herd of predators, and as loving as Estreya, who celebrates every morning and every encounter as if taken by surprise, as if he knew it could have been otherwise. My little dog knows that chance and death are more dangerous than gunpowder; he knows they can strike with the force of a sudden storm.

British Science

Suddenly everything goes still, the wide pastures – that usually ripple and wave – stop their swaying, a heavy silence descends over everything, a black thunder cloud that had seemed far off is right overhead, imminent in an instant, billowing, swollen, whorls of mottled grey. Although its texture might appear soft to the eyes of those of us on the ground below, in the short time it would take us to get the jerky into the wagon, a torrent of rain would pour down on us, and violent lightning would flash, striking trees and sometimes animals. Liz kept a scientific object in the wagon called a Franklin rod. When a storm broke she would run and stick one end on the roof and poke the other into the mud. It worked. Lightning could strike like bombs all around us and we were safe like under an umbrella. I loved umbrellas: there were two in the wagon. One got lost during one of my experiments. I'd wanted to try and use it against the wind, and before that I'd used it as a bag to carry grass to my cow, the one I started milking when Rosario arrived. I'd also used it as a vessel: I'd tried to fill it with water to see if it would work as a container. Our gaucho had woven a little straw roof over the wagon seat and he sheltered there with Estreya whenever it rained, when the sky was a bulging mass of different greys, the thick light livid and sickly, and everything blue became almost black, like it was conspiring to flatten us. Liz and I would scramble inside, sodden, our clothes stuck to our bodies, hair dripping down our faces, feet swimming around in our shoes. We rarely had time to find the lamps. Before the storm, what hung in the air, and even the air itself, seemed to be the long inhalation of the bellows of a machine priming itself for an explosion, or the stampede of a herd of captive beasts. Invariably after the stillness a commotion would begin. Everything yielded to the violence of the wind that took advantage of the sudden darkness to lash the world, a world barely visible in the metallic flashes that struck everything that stood upright, drawing a new line from the lines in the sky down to the earth: a line making everything crack, split and fly off in fury, as if reluctantly snatched from stillness. Because stillness is the natural state of the pampa; activity takes place mainly below ground, in that humus that is both substance and a continent, that is more womb than anything else. Argentina is a land of botanical adventure; the most important thing that happens there happens to the seed, it happens unseen and unheard, it happens in that primordial mud from which we come and to which we surely go: the seed down in the darkness is swollen with moisture, dodging cuys and vizcachas it sprouts a stem, it grows a green leaf, it pushes its way through the bowels of the earth, it emerges under orders from its two seed-leaves until it manages to get enough energy from the sun and water so it doesn't need those leaves any more, and right then and there a cow appears and gobbles up that little blade of grass that was born in the ground and the cow reproduces, and slowly and surely multiplies into generations of animals that will end up, almost all of them, being slaughtered. Their blood will fall to the earth where the seeds lie, and their bones will make a delicious skeleton for the caranchos and worms, and their flesh will be refrigerated and shipped to Great Britain, another vein, bloody and frozen, in this network of veins that runs from all over the world to the voracious heart of the Empire. Argentina plays the part of the womb in all this. Unseen and unheard processes, like I said, invisible, connected to the magma of all beginnings and all endings. Great Britain is a whole other story. It is the isle of iron and steam, of know-how, it is the island built on the work of men, not on the work of the soil and animal flesh.

Flesh, the flesh is so weak, so prone to violent twists of fate, like the storms that came upon us almost without warning in the desert. Both of us would get in the wagon and take off our clothes, dry ourselves with those towels from the mills of Lancashire, that before that had come from the Mississippi Delta and from the cracks of the whip on the backs of black people in the United States; almost everything that I touched knew more about the world than I did, and was new to me. The thick towels with their soft threads, that wrapped and enfolded us, and then a nightgown and woolly blankets and the cow hides, and the glow of a little tallow candle; the dim brownish yellow light streaked silver by flashes of lightning and the sound of the wind and rain. I would lean against Liz and she would read aloud. On one of those nights, the very first stormy night I think, though all my memories of that journey are tinged with the aura of newness and it can't really have been a succession of first times; though perhaps it was, and I was reborn in the same pampa where I'd been born fourteen or fifteen years before, in any case, that night the wagon shook in the storm and Liz began to read *Frankenstein,* a story about a monster made of corpses and lightning. He was a poor monster with no father or mother, a poor forsaken monster made by British science with lightning, just like the lightning that was striking like bombs all around us right then, and which, steered by an apparatus like our Franklin rod, was called electricity. I felt a new kind of terror that night. Estreya smelt it, he jumped into the wagon and began licking my face. Rosario asked what was going on; being a tracker he too could smell the fear. I told him the story of the monster and he began shouting from outside the wagon that it couldn't be true, that what Liz had read to me was pure lies, that only God could create life, not some gringo with a flash of lightning. But if it wasn't a load of old cobblers, then you could probably make new animals too. Liz invited him in and poured three whiskies, then three more, and then three more again. Rosario, by then I was calling him Rosa and he was Rose to Liz, dreamt up a cow with the legs of a ñandú and the head of a puma, so that it could defend itself or at least run away. Sheep with duck feet so that they could cross rivers without too much trouble. Horses that grew wool for the winter. Cow trees. Like sheep trees, said Liz: when cotton – the same as in the towels – was first brought to Europe, people thought that sheep sprouted in gigantic trees on branches so strong and flexible that the hanging fruit could merrily nibble the grass. 'More cobblers, like that gaucho made of dead men and lightning,' concluded Rosario in delight just before he nodded off. Liz let him sleep inside, as well as Estreya, who had got into bed with us. She gave me a kiss on the forehead. I hugged her and fell asleep wondering if dragons weren't also animals made by British scientific experiments with electricity and promising myself that I would do everything I could to find out. I fell asleep rather proud of my scientific curiosity, me, who until then couldn't tell Sunday from Wednesday or January from July. I'd rarely been so happy in my life.

Suspended in the Air

When I woke up late, startled by so much light – I was usually up and about before dawn – the wagon was humid, hot as an oven, and, unusually, three or four flies were buzzing around and landing on my face. I shooed them away. The electric monsters had given me nightmares: sheep with red eyes shooting lightning bolts at me and baring their hyena-teeth. The leader of the flock, a black sheep with blue horns and countless teeth, its mouth like a forest of white knives, came towards me and just as it opened up its jaws to swallow me I woke up. I was terrified, my heart was beating so loud I thought everyone would hear it. But no. Rosa was snoring loudly, Liz more softly. Only Estreya noticed, he rolled onto me and went back to sleep. His gentle breathing and the rhythm of his little heart on top of mine gradually spread to me, and I calmed down. I lay there a while listening to the drops of rain on the cover of the wagon. The sheep had reminded me how terrified I was of having to return to my old life and it made me think about La Negra. The woman who raised me was every bit as vicious, despite having no horns and practically no teeth. She was born furious. She used to whip me or beat me with a stick on a daily basis, whether or not I'd been disobedient. My back still bears the scars. How did I end up in her hands? I asked myself all over again. What had happened to my mother and father? There's always a mother and a father, except in Frankenstein's case. And I just lay there completely amazed at myself: why had it never occurred to me to look for them? When I was really little La Negra told me that she'd found me in a trunk by her door. She had a shiny wooden trunk in the house that was much nicer than anything else in the entire settlement. I would climb into it along with some beef jerky and water, close the lid, and stay in there nice and still, until even my breath slowed. And there I would wait. I did the closest thing I knew to praying: I talked to that God I'd heard a bit about and I would ask him to get me out of there. I repeated this prayer: 'Get me out of here, please, Mister God; get me out of here Mister God, please; please Mister God, Mister God our Father, get me out of here.' Or I'd convince myself that the trunk was my house and that my parents would come back to find me and they'd look for me inside it, and if I wasn't there they might go away again. So I got inside it whenever I got the chance, every time El Negro and La Negra weren't paying attention, every time they got to drinking caña at the general store and collapsed in a drunken heap. Whenever she found me there, La Negra would pull me out by my hair and tan my hide for being lazy, as she saw it. When I got a bit bigger I held on to my fantasy: La Negra would laugh at me saying that my mother must be one of those foreign women who ended up working as whores for the estancia bosses. That night, with Estreya on top of me, Liz next to me, and Rosa a few yards away, so far away from there, I asked myself if God had heard my crying, the way I used to cry in the days when I still cried: crying my eyes out completely silently. My tears were like the swollen rivers back there: pure silent water. I thought about the whole boss's whore thing. It had never occurred to me: I might be a boss's daughter. I decided I'd look into that first, and then into the dragon question. I was learning: Liz had told me that order is essential and you should take things one at a time. I fell peacefully asleep.

There was still a bit of hot tea left when I climbed out of the wagon. Rosa was good with fires: there wasn't a dry branch, or dry anything, for miles around. And one of the wagon wheels was stuck two or three feet down in the mud: it had come off the terra firma of the Indian trail. There was boundless life in the desert; a world of burrows lay under the ground, a labyrinth of deep and shallow tunnels, sometimes parallel, sometimes crossing. Up until more or less the time of the journey that I'm telling you about, that vast territory was uncultivated, but maybe because of how well these underground tunnels ventilated the roots of everything planted there, it later produced fabulous harvests.

Vizcachas are hardworking animals that use their little paws like human hands and dig deep store cupboards for their provisions: tender shoots, grass, roots, seeds, any fruit they happen to find. When one of these stores is underneath a cuy burrow an enormous cross shape forms that, in the unlikely event of a wagon going over it, ends up collapsing and the wagon falls into a muddy pit of squashed baby cuy guts. That noon you could see the poor creatures swimming in their flooded burrows, carrying in their teeth the young who had survived. Back and forth they went, trying to save them. The muddy landscape stretched out showing its innards, its network of tunnels and caves, some deep, some not so deep, some straight, some crooked, all criss-crossing one another. Every step was a struggle, you had to haul your feet out of the mud.

Liz and Rosa were exhausted: we wouldn't be able to get going again until the road dried up a bit, the cattle were bellowing as they sank into the mud, even the horses, usually so bold, hung back, finding their footing.

And we were all getting bitten by horse flies. But birds had appeared: filling the sky with sound, bathing noisily in the pools of water, as if they were born from water, as if their life was in waiting until they got wet, as if somehow their lives were part of the cycle of seeds. And the cicadas, the frogs and the toads chirruped and croaked in chorus, thanking the sky for their rainbath. Bees hung in the steam rising from the sun-warmed mud. They didn't go anywhere, just stayed buzzing, suspended in the air. Summer was bursting forth.

We could see an ombú in the distance and something that looked like a stream a bit further on. Having an order of priority, father-dragons, made me clear-headed: I suggested we wash, eat, have a siesta under the ombú and then set off at dusk. It was quite feasible: the Indian trail seemed solid enough, we just had to be on the look-out. First we gathered grass. Lots, all soggy, then we chopped it up with the machete and fed it to the cows who were going crazy in the mud; they'd need energy to set off in a few hours' time. Afterwards we set up under the tree, brewed more tea, and Liz produced a honey cake; there was a whole world inside that wagon, it seemed limitless, and we had the longest breakfast I'd ever had. I told them my plans. The one about the dragon made Liz laugh, but tracking down my father who might be a landowner seemed sensible to her: that kind of thing goes on all the time, she told me. She reeled off lots of examples, and ended up going back to the wagon to look for a book. She brought out *Oliver Twist* and began reading it out: he was an English orphan whose luck changed when he found his family. You could tell he was of high birth from his impeccable morals, she said. I would find my family. Or maybe I'd already found it. That's right, Liz said to me, stroking my hair, but there is another one: your birth family. I still haven't found that one.

We Branded Each and Every Animal

We set off at sundown: I won't dwell on it, I won't keep going on about the light or about how it softened everything, even the weeds that moments before had been rough and prickly, despite their flowers. Back then the pampa was a mass of thistles, their purple crowns taller than a grown man: from our perch on the wagon, the purple land rippled gently. The oxen, who led the way, ended up as flowery and thorny as the thistles themselves, they were four-legged plants, cow-cactuses, animals like the ones made by scientists, Rosa said. He groomed them because they deserved it, and I think the oxen loved him for that; they tended to follow him around a bit when he unyoked them. Otherwise, they seemed pretty indifferent to most things. Probably because of the weight of the yoke, poor creatures, dulled by work. We made our way silently following the subtle traces left by the passage of the Indian hordes, traces already getting overgrown with thistles. The Indians trod lightly like cats, with characteristic stealth and suddenness, leaving almost nothing behind. We were a bit afraid of them, but only a bit: Rosa was there, and he was half Indian, he said. He didn't look it, he was white with a single eyebrow; he looked more Spanish, he was so hairy he looked like a Spanish cuy and he was very hardworking, his hands were never idle. He was only half Indian, his father's mother was Guaraní and he spoke her language and could use it to bellow out a sapukái, as he proceeded to demonstrate: his eyes watered, the veins bulged on his neck, his face went red, and he howled, scattering the real cuys, sending the chimangos skywards, petrifying the cattle, cracking Liz's face open with horror, and making Estreya bark himself hoarse at this sudden stranger; apparently it was a good sapukái. Rosa in full battle cry was really quite frightening, he transformed into someone else, the man with the gaucho knife, the man he claimed to be. There wasn't much point in us explaining to him that we were heading for Tehuelche territory; he was convinced all Indians could understand one another, so it was no use arguing. It wasn't the Indians, but the fort he was afraid of. He'd deserted a while back. How long ago? He said he didn't really have much sense of time, but several summers and winters had passed, he'd come down from the north rounding up all the cattle he came across. Liz and I reckoned it must have been about ten years before. We wanted to keep the cows, we could make cheese, Liz said, who was convinced that prosperity only came to those who worked for it. She came up with a good ruse: we could brand all the cattle with the mark of the landowner who had sent Liz and the Gringo to Argentina to oversee his estancia. There was just one problem: we had no branding iron. I found one of those big rings which held up the wagon axles. It seemed just the job and we branded each and every animal. All three hundred and forty-seven of them. Needless to say we made slow progress: the cows, the wagon, the lack of a proper track apart from the Indian trail, which was easier on horseback, with the threat of a quaghole or vizcacha burrows at every step. Nothing helped us, least of all me. I didn't want to get there. I wanted to live in the wagon forever, in this suspended interval of time, just the four of us without the Englishman; I wanted Liz without her husband, I wanted, I didn't know what I wanted, I wanted her to love me, to find life impossible without me, to hold me tight, I wanted the pillow beside hers to be mine. I spun the animal branding out over three days, with ever-longer siestas, I plied everyone with plentiful whiskies from the three barrels in the wagon, I asked them questions so they would tell stories. Fear paralysed me: the wagon was like my childhood trunk if the trunk could have grown wheels and some friends had come along. It was another world, one that was truly mine. Everything else was a threat – La Negra, life with Fierro, that shack, cowering silently from all the brutality I'd suffered: no one there had anything to say except about land and meat, going on about cows, rain and drought, gossiping about which farmhand was mounting what girl, and whether so-and-so's children were also his brothers and sisters as well as his father's children and grandchildren, wondering whether the owner of the estancia would come or not, if he was coming whether he'd punish or reward, and whether or not there'd be another Indian raid. There wasn't, they'd already pushed the Indians further and further towards to the desert, to where we were now. The old folk remembered how things had been before, when the Indians would appear like a whirlwind and leave everything dead behind them. They were worse than a plague of locusts: they killed men, cows, even dogs. It was said the reason there was no church was because they'd burnt it down with the people still inside. One of the old men, the one who had taken in my children, was a boy when it happened and he saw the whole thing from up a tree. He heard the screams, smelled the burning flesh, and waited, muted and frozen with fear, on the top branch for the divine lightning bolt that would strike down the heathens. He was up there for two days, and in the end he climbed down, absolutely terrified, but assuming that, for the moment at least, the Indians wouldn't come back because there was nothing left to steal or kill. And convinced that the lightning bolt of God would have struck them down in the desert. He went to the fort and stayed there until the old guy from the big house returned and took him back, along with a couple of gauchos he'd brought together with the new cows, those beautiful white cows with reddish-brown patches which is how I remember cows being when I was little: English cattle that had been herded onto a ship. Most of the old folk I'd met had arrived after the times of the Indian raids. The Indians didn't know how to speak, they used to say. They just howled like wild beasts, tore things apart like pumas, knew neither God nor pity, raped women because they had no notion of affection, they even made stew with white folks' babies because they were more tender than their own: the darker they are, the tougher they are – it's a well-known fact, said the gauchos, who also prided themselves on being tough; they were dark and macho, not like those lily-livered landowners, they said. That's why they did the kind of job they did, because they were macho and tough. They laughed imagining the landowner's blond fair-skinned son trying to round up cattle, break in a horse or bring down a ñandú with a swing of the bolas; they hadn't lived under the dictator Juan Manuel de Rosas, nor the first owner of the estancia. The sons of the landowners spent their time in France, and on their rare visits, the gauchos treated them reverently, bowing to them, and calling them sir, if they'd had a tail it would've been between their legs. But curiously the gauchos were certain that in a one-to-one fight they'd win. And generally speaking they were right; if they'd fought with knives, the gaucho would've walked away unscathed. Or galloped away! quipped Rosa, who in the early hours after plenty of whisky regaled us with his story as if yielding to a lover: he bared his soul to us.

An Orphan's Fate

Rosa's fate was an orphan's fate too: he left his mother's house with his face streaming with blood. He didn't want to abandon her but he realised that his stepfather would end up killing him the next time they had a run-in. So the young gaucho left home with nothing for company but his knife and Bizco, his young horse. He thinks he wandered for days: he doesn't remember much, his face throbbed, flies were buzzing round his wound and he was blinded by the fierce Corrientes sun. He fainted. How or why he has no idea, but his horse didn't head for home; instead it carried on slowly, perhaps aware of its fragile load, until it reached an estancia. He was found by some gauchos, who took him in, and an old woman cured his wound with herbs, poultices and words he's since forgotten. Once he could speak, he told her all his misfortunes and the old woman took pity on him, made space for him in her hovel, gave him an animal hide to lie on, and allowed him to bed down by the fire. The old woman lived alone; her husband had died and her son had gone off with the militia. She eked out a living by growing squashes and manioc, helped by the charity of the foreman. Her luck turned with Rosa; although he was still just a boy, he was already skilled at horse-taming and he began working with the stock. They were already giving him the wildest horses to break in before he'd even got hairs on his chin. Rosa never beat the horses, he talked to them, stroking their necks. 'I had my own tech-nique', he said, savouring the word as though it was a delicacy; he'd had a bit of trouble learning it and he pronounced it like someone presenting a golden cigar box, or a costly precious jewel, some kind of crown. The gauchos had been amazed by his technique, they thought that Rosa was casting spells on the horses and when they got very drunk they started pestering him. They asked him to teach them; they wouldn't believe it was just a matter of talking slowly and putting an arm round the horse's neck. They threatened to chuck him into the corral with all the most dangerous bulls to see if he could make them sweet-tempered too, and none of his explanations would satisfy them. They couldn't believe he'd got a tech-nique that anyone could use, Rosa told us. By then he had a girlfriend, María the little china was called, she had the longest plaits of anyone in the huts, she fried little pancakes, spoke softly to him, could tell stories, and liked going with him to the marshes. Rosa had made a raft to row among the water hyacinths, and they played around poking caimans in the mouth with sticks. Long sticks, of course, from a distance, and it wasn't a game they played often. It was quite a sight to see a caiman swallowing an unwary heron in one gulp, and they could easily flip the raft over if they felt like it. But they didn't. He and María went to the islands on their raft and it was all laughter and kissing. He had his love, he had the old woman who he was very fond of, he had his little horse Bizco, who only he could ride. And he planned to go home to his mother some day and free her from that bastard of a gaucho. At this point in the story, the owner returned. He was old with a long yellowing beard, he looked like the sun and he was a good man. He paid their over-due wages, gave them half a cow to roast and chocolate to drink, he struck up on his guitar, and there was dancing; everyone there – boys, girls, parrots, macaws, cows, horses, toads, lapwings and crickets – all shouted three cheers for the boss! He brought his son along, the young master, who was also fair-haired and seemed delicate; he wore glasses and although you never saw a gaucho with glasses, his father wanted to make a man of him. The cattle herders took him out with them: they taught him to swing the bolas, to use a lasso, to hunt, to cross rivers on horseback, to keep going in the rain, to endure the sun and to fight. He always won, because they let him. The old boss liked Rosa's way of working with the horses because he didn't hurt them; 'you've got a technique', he said and that's how Rosa learnt to name his talent, 'teach it to my son'. Rosa showed him, but soon realised that the blond boy couldn't do it, however hard Rosa tried; he couldn't learn, so Rosa spent his nights taming the wild horses and the other boy was happy in the morning, priding himself on having a technique of his own. The boy asked Rosa to take him out on the raft. Rosa warned him about the caimans but the young master said no problem, took two pistols along and they came back dragging two huge creatures behind them, roasted them on a spit, and they were great. He brought wine and they drank it, ending up arm in arm like the best of friends, and from then on they galloped together all over his father's land. The young master always had to come first and as long as he did, peace reigned. One afternoon, having downed a fair amount of caña, he got it into his head that he wanted to ride Bizco. Rosa said no, explaining that only he could mount Bizco; Bizco was his horse, Bizco had saved his life and he loved him, Bizco was all that he had left to him from his mother. The blond boy said that if an orphan could ride Bizco, he could too. He mounted: Rosa spoke softly into the horse's ear, persuading him not to resist. The horse walked on, and things seemed to be going smoothly until the blond boy started cracking the whip. Bizco whinnied, reared up like a demon and threw him off. Rosa went running to pick him up; the horse was still quite close by, so the young master got back on and really laid into him with the whip. Bizco threw him off again, the young master got to his feet, grabbed the reins, drew his knife and slashed the horse's throat. Rosa could still remember the horse's eyes, how the poor beast looked pleadingly at him when it was already too late, and Rosa flew at the young master and beat him to a pulp. The bastard cried like a girl, the other gauchos came to rescue him and set upon Rosa, who came round to find himself bound hand and foot to four stakes in the ground. The young master came along presently and stood over him, 'so you thought you could beat me up, you fucking Indian?' and he took out his prick and pissed on him. The other gauchos laughed half-heartedly, like when they let him win. At night they took pity on Rosa, and when it was pitch black they freed him. He took the best horse and made his escape. He hid in dense scrub, his body aching from the stakes. They came searching for him, but since the young master was the only one who really wanted to find him, he stayed hidden till they forgot all about it or gave him up for lost. Rosa lay in wait for him, and as soon as he galloped past alone, Rosa attacked him. 'We fell to the ground. He took his pistol out and shot at me. He got me, but I could still use my knife. I stuck it in him. I caught him in the shoulder, then pulled it out and gave him a new smile across his neck. I left him where he lay, spat on him and pissed on him. Then I galloped off.' Once again alone and wounded, with nothing but his horse and his knife, he set off on his way, only this time in the opposite direction: Rosa was headed home. His dear mother began crying the minute she set eyes on him, begging him to leave, and his brothers and sisters cried too for fear of their stepfather's fury. Rosa ordered them to get outside and hide behind the trees. His mother pleaded with him not to do anything, said things weren't so terrible, and who would feed them all, and that she was worried that he, her dear son, would get killed. Rosa didn't listen. He sat himself down in the shack with his mother's pot of stew bubbling away. His stepfather came in, asked 'Where is everyone? What are you doing here you Guaraní piece of shit? What do you want? I'm looking for you, you Indian bastard.' 'Me, an Indian?' exclaimed the older man taking his knife out, 'draw your knife and we'll see who's boss.' Rosa drew his knife, they circled around the pot, facing each other. The old man struck at Rosa's chest: Rosa dodged the blade and pushed the old man over. Then Rosa jumped on him, hauled him over, sat on his backside as if he was riding him, grabbed his hair and shouted you bastard, you beat my mother, you cut my face, and you hurt my brothers and sisters, and he slashed the man's throat from top to bottom. He felt the man die, felt every last shudder of life ebbing out of that hateful body, which gradually slackened as the blood soaked away into the animal hide beneath. Rosa got to his feet and dragged the body outside, took out the hide to cover it up, shouted to his mother to come inside and feed his siblings, then dragged the old man's body about a league into the marshland and threw him close to four caimans. He saw the animals rouse themselves from their lethargy and creep slowly forwards, knowing their prey wouldn't run away. They ate the body. Rosa went back home, bid farewell to his mother, told his next oldest brother that it was his turn to be the man of the house, and rode off like someone whose lifeblood is draining away: he left never to return.

I Was Burning My Bridges

They're cow parasites, cattle lice, Liz said to me one day. She was talking about gauchos in the same dispassionate tone as she had when she told me that strawberries were red; her voice was perfectly neutral. They're horse flies too, I added, without hiding my scorn: I was burning my bridges. To leave you have to become another person. I'm not sure how I knew that, I was still so young then; I was leaving with the speed and force of a locomotive, one of those machines I'd sworn to myself I would see, and that I would indeed see one day advancing over pastureland and Indian settlements, pampa and mountains. I was becoming someone else and was leaving behind those who'd been mine: first La Negra, who had treated me roughly but also had her soft side. I can still remember her looking after me when I was very small. I remember a lullaby. I remember cool cloths on my forehead and poultices on my chest. And I had clothes and food and a language to speak and a house, if that's what you can call those shacks made from mud and dung, with nothing for furniture but a pile of animal skins and bones: the leftovers from an asado. Yes, Liz – who believed in work more than in God the Father – was right about gauchos being parasites on cows and horses. She was right about my people's life of meat and water; we didn't grow squashes or beans, we didn't weave or fish, we barely hunted, didn't use any wood other than fallen branches, and then only to make fire. We lived in a kind of stupor, sitting on the skulls of bulls and horses, wearing boots made from horses' hooves, eating meat morning, noon and night, going to trade animal skins for caña, mate and tobacco in the general store, rounding up or branding cattle. We all used to sleep in a heap, on top of one another, writhing like a mound of larvae, under cattle hides in winter or near a fire made from dry sticks and cow and horse dung to ward off the mosquitoes in summer. In a heap. All of us. Pricks and cunts oozing with no regard for familial ties or taboos, just like a seething mass of larvae. I think La Negra started punishing me for that, when El Negro started to paw at me; she did it out of jealousy – even animals get jealous. I used to steer clear of him, I was scared of that toothless black drunkard from the day he arrived in the house and I tried to cling to her but she swore at me and hit me, so I began to stay away from the fire and put sticks beside me, hoping that if El Negro came near me, the sticks would fall over because he wouldn't see them in the dark in his drunken state. I hid away with another orphan, a half-Indian boy who had ended up in the huts with us when his mother died. She'd been on her way to Buenos Aires and had fallen as she walked with the baby boy on her back. The gauchos found her unconscious and took her in out of pity. There was nothing they could do for her: she told them she'd escaped from the Indians and she wanted to go back to her family. She pleaded with them to take her boy to the city, and as she talked her face got paler and paler, until that was it. The poor boy just stayed there; they threw food to him, and he wandered from shack to shack like a stray dog, trying to fit in and make himself useful. It was in looking for shelter that he picked up the gaucho ways: he'd fetch and carry water, could light a fire even in a storm, and would fight with a puma if required. In the end he got noticed by the foreman, who decided he was slightly less larval than the rest of them, and taught him to work. He taught him metalworking, how to cut firewood from the few scrawny trees, and to look after the boss's fruit trees. Raúl was his name, and when I fled from the Negros I got together with him. He was a sturdy little bull-necked gaucho with strong intelligent hands, a dazzling flash of beauty. He set traps with tree branches and we spread our animal skins out to lie on the grass. With him I knew what pleasure our bodies can bring, the sweet joy of being desired and celebrated. A couple of times El Negro, feeling cheated of his property, tried to stand up to Raúl, but he was old by then. And Raúl was a good man. He hardly grazed El Negro's face. He ought to have killed him, I thought then, and I was right to think so: the old bastard put me up as the prize in a card game and Fierro beat him and between the two of them they dragged me to church by the hair, knackering two horses on the way, and married me off. I stopped speaking. There was nothing that could be done. Raúl looked at me from a distance and I looked back at him, and when my first child was born, Fierro saw he had Indian features. Fierro, who'd never seen himself in a mirror, and who only turned up two days after the birth, up to the eyeballs in caña. By early the next morning my beloved Raúl was dead, with his head split in two like a canyon. He must have been drinking and fallen over, people said. We all knew that wasn't true. Raúl didn't drink. By the time the foreman came back, we'd already moved on to another settlement. And although the foreman was very fond of Raúl, he wasn't flesh and blood.

Fierro killed my Raúl, but I think he didn't kill me because I was the only blonde china he'd touched in his life and I was his; that set him apart from the other men, because I was a trophy worthy of a landowner. He took us to another estancia and he went off to work as a mule driver. Months later he turned up, tired and sober, and saw his son. The boy, like Fierro, has moles that form a star in his groin. I saw Fierro's eyes mist up and he spoke tenderly to me. I didn't answer. I could never love that drunken bastard Fierro. I'd never been able to, and even less so after he killed my Raúl. Thankfully I didn't see much of him. I was careful not to let anyone touch me and he didn't touch me much either. Open up, he'd say every now and then, there'd be a few brief shudders inside me, then off he'd go. When he wasn't driving his mules he was drinking at the general store or he was flat out on the ground asleep like the rest of them. I was drunk and I just kipped where I fell, he'd say. I didn't care where he fell, as long as it wasn't anywhere near me. When he did lie beside me, I thought about killing him, one night I grabbed his knife to bring it down hard on the back of his neck and at that point a thought occurred to me that made me freeze: where would I go? I stood stock still, the very effigy of a murderer: all the weight of the image of two hands brandishing the knife behind the head, back bent, breath held. I'd like to be able to say that a shaft of moonlight glinted off the blade, but I can't. Everything about Fierro was filthy, even his knife.

I didn't have to kill him, they took him away. And I left without knowing where I was going. I betrayed him too. The only person I never betrayed was Raúl: we'd always planned to escape together.

A Prophet with a Paintbrush

Of Liz's origins we knew less, only the little she told us: unlike me, she did have a father and mother, Scottish farmers, both redheads like her. Her father was a farmer more by accident than design. He'd wanted to be an artist and, to be fair, that's what he was; he spent more time with his canvases than digging potatoes. His wife grumbled, exhausted, what with the vegetable garden and the children to look after, but she loved him and wanted him to paint; she was dazzled by his landscapes, with their diffuse blocks of light, the light of the Lord Jesus – as she saw it – believing the father of her children to be a prophet with a paintbrush. And in a way he was, says Liz, he thought that God was made of something a bit like the sun and he explained the world to her as blocks of colours. Even in complete darkness, when it seems as though He isn't there, and we feel utterly abandoned, it's just a matter of looking really hard: something will shine, something will guide us, we have to keep going and look for a spark. Her father would find those sparks in the livid aura around swirling Scottish clouds and piles of potato peelings, their outlines shining brightly; whirlwinds of shorn wool like fireflies against the cottony whiteness of a shifting sky. White on white was something old Mr Scott knew how to paint, and you could easily distinguish one white from another at a glance; he also knew how to depict the sun at its zenith, diffusing sea and pastures. He was a rustic Turner, Liz explained to me as she unrolled a few of her father's canvases, and I understood what she meant by blocks of light, of course I did coming from the pampas, but I didn't know what she meant by Turner, so she took out another canvas, *Snow Storm – Steam-Boat off a Harbour's Mouth*. It was a copy that her father had made to sell back home in his village. She then got out another one, which made an even bigger impression on me: a locomotive, black and ferocious, emerging from the slightly translucent yet thick orange light of dawn breaking over a river. You could just make out a little rowing boat; it's Maidenhead Bridge on the River Thames, Liz said to me, a triumph of the Industrial Revolution, just like the locomotive that's travelling westward from London. The painting was called *Rain, Steam and Speed – The Great Western Railway*. The sky is thick because of smog, Liz explained to me: the air in London was dirty, it had specks of coal floating in it and those tiny particles did two things at once: they refracted and multiplied the dawn, and they made the air grimy. Turner was our prophet too. I liked all that light, her father Bruce Scott's light, William Turner's light with his locomotive and his little boat, a light that was so much like ours, yet so far away. I could feel that light inside me, in all of us and in everything we did out in the open air of the pampas, which was so much clearer, I thought, than the air in England. And I was right. I wanted to paint; Liz knew how, and so I got started.

Brush in hand, fascinated by the palette of water-colours, I tried to paint the two of us with our oxen. It didn't turn out that bad. Liz continued talking; she used to be as happy as anything going on walks with her father, and they would talk about life, about the books he got her to read, about her school, about what the future might hold. That future suddenly became clear when she met Oscar: she decided to leave to make her fortune in the far-off pampas. She didn't know much about them, just that they were almost virgin territory, there for the taking. Her father urged her to go, telling her to follow that new American light and then come back to Scotland; he would be waiting for her. And there she was, guiding my hand that trembled from her touch, under the blue sky of that new world, going to look for the fortune that was hers and that would save her mother from the farm, save her father from everything that wasn't painting, save her sisters from marriages not of their choosing, and save her brothers from the potatoes and from the British weather that was cold and miserable all year round.

When Liz tired of talking she kissed me very softly, and this time I dared to slowly brush my tongue over her lips, slowly run my tongue over her tongue, aflame like Turner's locomotive in the blaze of a London dawn. She pushed me away, oh so gently, and told me to keep going with the watercolour, it was going well.

PART TWO

THE FORT

Dressed to the Nines

Estreya would bring us his finds: he'd drop bones at our feet and sit wagging his tail proudly, as if bestowing gold upon us. With a little shiver at the idea our own skeletons could meet the same fate, we stroked his head, we embraced, we loved each other all the more amidst the stench of death in the vicinity of the fort. Our love grew stronger as we realised our precarious situation, our fragility heightening our desire. We began sleeping by the fire all together so as to keep watch permanently, something that was becoming more and more difficult as the year wore on: the nights grew longer, as did the shadows during the day. Liz had title deeds that certified ownership of the land she was heading for, letters sealed by the English aristocrat who'd sent her, and a document from Buenos Aires authorising the letters, but the question on our minds was, how could we be sure those savages in the Argentine Army actually know how to read? And even if they do know, we can't be sure they won't steal the deeds and kill us all. Early one morning Estreya woke us with a howl. Rosa and I went to see what the dog was trying to show us: it was six fresh Indian corpses with about six thousand chimangos picking at them and at each other, squabbling over the best bits. In short, the four men, one woman, and one child were now little more than carrion for the birds.

We didn't dwell on it. Forcefully, Liz took charge. We mustn't let ourselves be taken by surprise; not only were we a British delegation, we also had to look the part. We had to follow protocol. She ordered us to change: Liz was a lady, I was a young Englishman, Rosa was a servant in proper uniform – there were even uniforms in the wagon, uniforms for every kind of position on the estancia according to the imagination of the aristocrat and his stewards, Liz and Oscar. Dressed to the nines, we travelled past that feeding ground for chimangos; me in my frock coat, Liz in her dress, and Rosa in his uniform, so much fancier than anything we'd see later.

A Dust Cloud Can Linger

Under the piercingly hot rays, a cloud of earth was hanging between the ground and the clear blue sky: we arrived at noon on one of the last days of summer. A dust cloud can linger, it can seem as much a part of the sky as the sun and the chimangos. But beware, raised dust means movement and movement means danger: you need to be able to figure out who or what is causing it, stopping it from falling back to the ground, keeping it in the air in defiance of gravity. Rosa rode out in front, bolt upright in his uniform and astride his British saddle, that horrible thing he called it, even though it was obvious he felt much more secure in that attire, if a bit uncomfortable, half choked by the stiff collar, and seated atop that artefact that hindered his movements. Jogging along, he looked like an army general. He stopped just short of the cloud and a few moments later the curtain of dust in front of him cleared a little. That's when we understood where the animals were coming from: all kinds of worms, grubs, cuys, hares, partridges, rats, vizcachas, assorted armadillos, ñandús, red deer, pumas, and wild boar hurtled towards us tracing bullet-straight lines before vanishing again into the nothingness of the pampa. When the dust had settled a bit more, and we saw the terracotta heads of gauchos appearing out of a ditch with a mountain of earth behind them, we realised what the line was that from up on the wagon we could see stretching across the horizon. The gauchos indicated the route to Rosa and went back to their digging. Now the line was unbroken. We could just make out a figure on horseback, a soldier as dirty as the gauchos. He spoke to someone, surveyed the wagon, paused, and then rode off at a trot, presumably to inform someone of our arrival. Rosa came back to us, dismounted, requested a brush and set about smartening up his uniform, saddle and horse. Let's go, said Liz, and we set off for the entrance of the fort. The fort was called Las Hortensias, though it didn't deserve a name that evoked a flower in any sense.

Do Come In, My Dear

We were led through the fort to the main building. It was huge, spotlessly white, and glossy like the hide of a strong, healthy animal. It had a veranda around it, floors that were so highly polished I was afraid of slipping over, a garden full of flowers and birdsong, and a covered well. In the middle of the garden there was a chair covered with red fabric. Once I had touched that fabric I couldn't leave it alone; its threads were short, and if I stroked it one way the colour was darker, the other way and it became lighter, and it was so smooth. Sitting right there waiting for us was the Colonel. The moment he saw us he stood up. He bowed. He kissed Liz's hand and began speaking to her. Within two words he knew she was British and pronounced himself delighted to be conversing with someone born in a nation so great as fair Albion's estate, slipping effortlessly into rhyming English. Liz presented him with the copy her father had made of Turner's locomotive painting; the Colonel's joy knew no bounds in either language. It's as if, he said, you knew that my purpose in life is to bring trains, the engines of progress, to Argentina. Do come in, my dear, I shall have you shown to your rooms, make yourselves at home, I'll have a bath filled for you to rinse off the dust of the pampas, there's a room for your brother too, do please make your way along. Then he turned to one of his servant girls: china! Take the visitors to the guest rooms. No sooner had Liz stepped onto the parquet floor, onto the rugs, and seen the pictures on the walls, than she visibly revived like a drooping plant in the rain: she swelled and became radiant, her eyes, her skin, her teeth, everything about her shone. And I finally saw what she'd so often described to me: in a wooden box with a glass lid, which she told me was called a display case, there was a ring. And set in the middle of that ring was a diamond, the stone for which men kill. It was beautiful, as if all the purest water in the world were contained in a single drop, so light and strong.

Colours Became Detached
from Their Objects

Colours became detached from their objects and floated over them, obscuring them and leaving them behind like dead bodies, like broken eggshells impregnated with reds and whites. White, I could see the whiteness of Liz's skin rise above the dining table, above the delicacies Hernández had spread before us, above Hernández himself, who was holding forth about livestock farming being a form of civilisation nowadays, a profession requiring scientific methods and refined intelligence, above Hernández's voice rose the whiteness of Liz's skin, above the servants who were continually refilling our glasses, above the crockery – oh the crockery! that white porcelain with a blue design of a wood, a little house, a river, it was so lovely – above the jug and wash bowl, above the state of culture of a society that values equally a work of art and a machine, a woven cloth and a fleece, above the silver cutlery that was ranged on the table like a glittering arsenal and which I had no idea how to use, so I just copied Liz, the whiteness rose above me too as I ate salad when she ate it, cut up my bread when she cut hers, speared and cut the BeefWellington – red cow meat like the kind I was used to but surrounded by vegetables and encased in a sort of shell called puff pastry, the white of Liz's skin rose above the wine – oh the wine! – that day I tasted red wine for the first time and my pulse quickened and I began to see the white that floated above everything, above the glasses and bottles, above the whole room's dark mahogany panelling, above me, above the pink silk dress that she was wearing that had a boat neckline, no, a square neckline, a French gown, she explained to me and she'd already told me about France, a country full of elegant people and artists and women of easy virtue, she also had to explain to me what easy virtue was and how only women can have it, the pale gleam floated into every nook and cranny, the whiteness rose above Hernández's voice, which filled the room with its agricultural industries and the global population boom which clusters in particular places determined by their richness in natural resources, above the charms of social life, and above many other circumstances, above Liz herself I saw that whiteness, her cleavage and the roundness of her breasts which no dress could hide, her white skin radiated round the ranchowner's dining room together with the red in her flowing locks which reflected her breasts as a river reflects, those red swathes of hair that moved to different currents, like rows of millet blown this way and that by the winds, oh! all the factors that have made it imperative to develop our agriculture and livestock, Liz pushed her hair across her face, hiding and revealing it like a child playing peek-a-boo, now you see it, now you don't, which not only satisfy our basic needs, and her eyelids, her curved red eyelashes played the same game with her almost transparent blue eyes, those ghostly eyes of hers, and her hair fell over her bosom and my God! I was smitten, and the Colonel saying that it will also provide for the comfort and wellbeing of the working classes, and for the luxury of those who are well off, I was paralysed, and it was all I could do to raise my right hand and lift the wineglass to my lips, that white and that red had overshadowed all the other marvellous things I came to know that night, crystal wineglasses, the tablecloth embroidered with pheasants, flower vases brimming with flowers, wrought silver salvers, I was speechless, but then nobody expected me to speak, since Liz had introduced me as her little brother Joseph, Joseph Scott; the Colonel was getting worked up, bullish, I saw his back lengthen, his chest broaden, his beard become redder and curlier, he seemed to see what I saw, Liz moved like a puma that knows its own strength, Liz was a mighty beast, she was life itself displaying its finest flesh, its most alive and lively flesh, and the Colonel droned on about his cows, rural industry, about how barely thirty years before he'd seen the beacon of civilisation come to Argentina, Hernández talked about mares as he watched Liz shake out her mane, a chestnut mare rearing up on her hind legs, strong and burnished with white and red and pink as the old man carried on with his ode to progress in the pampas, progress that he was bringing, leaving behind the uncivilised ways of previous ranchers, they weren't a real industry, besides breaking in wild horses, it's so important to transform those wild animals into well-trained, useful animals he said, spittle drooling from his lips, and on he went, detailing the introduction of shorthorn bulls, English race horses, Friesian cattle, Rambouillet sheep and rams, the wonders of racial improvement with European breeds, and from there he jumped to the transformation that he personally was bringing about: we are transforming a seething mass of larvae into a workforce, just imagine, my dear, it won't be painless but nevertheless, we've had to sacrifice our compassion, we must all sacrifice ourselves in order to consolidate the Argentine Nation, he was saying, beginning to slur his words but speaking as forcefully as ever, he was physically expanding, Hernández was undergoing a volcanic eruption, his face began twitching, we are putting the music of civilisation into the flesh of these larvae, they will become a workforce whose hearts beat to the rhythm of the factory, our bugles play the rhythm of production to discipline their anarchic souls, he said, and his eyes began to wander, each in its own direction, then they sought each other out until he went cross-eyed, then he went purple, his eyeballs almost touching each other, and finally he roared: Everything else is savage, primitive and brutal! and the rural patriarch's head collapsed onto the table, his mouth spurting a strange kind of seed at us as he fell: a jet of vomit came out, his head split his plate in two, splashing the remains of the Beef Wellington with blood, glasses overturned, spreading wine across the tablecloth, the water jugs toppled and dripped over the edge of the table onto the floor, the liquid, like Hernández's words, leaving a sticky stain, and a pig's head intended for the third course leapt to the ground as if it were a bird or a kangaroo – yes, Liz had told me about them in the wagon too, there were kangaroos in the world like huge hares with a bag on their belly to carry their babies around, and they stood on two legs and moved in huge bounds.

I Climaxed Too

At that moment Liz stood up, called the manservant, and ordered him to take his master away and clean him up, then she called one of the chinas and instructed her to heat water for a bath, came over to me and took the wineglass from my hand, took my hand in hers and led me to her room, a huge bedroom with a huge bath, the bed was like a luxurious wagon without wheels, it even had a roof held up by carved wooden posts, and from this roof hung a canopy of the finest silk, golden and gauzy, suspended in airy folds like wisps of cloud. Needless to say I'd never set foot in a room like that before, I'd never seen anything but dirt-floored hovels where we lived and slept on animal skins, and the wagon, and now there was this bed that they called a four-poster, the silk, the gently flickering yellow of the oil lamps, an armchair, where I perched on the edge, intimidated by so many new things and by the red and white of Liz which carried on growing and expanding, until there was hardly anything left outside her dominion, and when she sat down beside me and those cool blue eyes of hers looked into mine, her power was absolute. Even more so when she pinned me against the armchair and kissed me at length, hours on end she kissed me, nobody had ever kissed me so much, and I came to know the warm, wet roughness of her tongue, her saliva spiralling between my teeth, her teeth on my lips, and I came to know more, I came to know so much that night when I first experienced wine and four-poster beds and bathtubs and crystal glasses and ranchers' ejaculations, I came to know those delicate smooth hands opening my shirt with deft strength, taking my breasts, caressing them gently at first, awakening desire, then squeezing them, rubbing them till it hurt, then sucking them, easing the pain she had caused, Liz sucked my nipples like a calf then bit them like a dog then went back to licking them, the way a baby lamb like Braulio would, and she kissed me again. And at last I recovered the ability to move and to do what I had been wanting to do for hours, to uncover her white cleavage, to place my hands between the silk of her dress and the skin of her breasts, pulling them out and resting them on my hands like the banquet had lain on the silver salvers, at dinner I copied her manners, now I mirrored her caresses, I licked her nipples, which were as pink as the pink silk of the dress she was still wearing until I plucked up the courage to start to undo it, but she grabbed my hands with unexpected strength and stood up, lifted me up and carried me to the bed, where she finished removing my trousers, all the while saying my Josephine and good boy and pushing her tongue into me as if to reassure me, to comfort me and also to lay claim to me, she stripped me naked, took her knickers off, and spread her skirt over me, caressing my whole body with its silk, before positioning herself on top of me, she rested the hollow of her cunt on the edge of mine and began moving back and forth, sliding on my slipperiness, on my sticky secret flesh, on my throbbing cunt, bubbling like boiling water, and I watched Liz from beneath as she swung back and the silk dress no longer covered my eyes, her breasts swaying, her neck arching back towards her heels, red hair cascading down her back almost to her waist, along the curve that began at her neck, her whole body went tense, even her cunt, and then she climaxed, melting into a puddle over me, pouring herself over me, she held me tight, finally allowing me to kiss her, she let me turn her over, face up on the bed, she let me spread her legs and put my fingers inside her, where she was all pink and red like the rest of her, and I felt that soft, wet muscular flesh and licked it, then she let me sit on top of her and find the right place for that new rocking motion, I gazed at her fair skin, I gazed into her clear blue eyes surrounded by red hair spilling over the pillow, and, at last, I climaxed too.

Tangled Legs

When I opened my eyes shortly afterwards – we'd hardly slept – Liz and I were interwoven, her red and my straw-coloured hair, her warm slightly bitter breath and mine probably similar, her large freckly breasts and mine the same but smaller, our tangled legs, and – judging by the sticky mass that stretched like elastic between the two of us – our crotches must have been pressed together all night. I'd barely stirred when my body began to rub against hers without my intervention, as if my body had its own plans. Rays of clear light were coming in through the shutters, traversing the shadows, and burnishing all the tiny specks that float in the air of rooms where the light filters in little by little. Just then there was a knock at the door and breakfast was announced. They had breakfast early on the estancia. Later I found out that getting up at the crack of dawn was a military custom, and it wasn't just decided by the activities or inactivities the day had in store. A deep kiss, enough to flood me down to my feet, was Liz's way of saying good morning, and then I sneaked off to my room to get dressed and to make sure I emerged through the right door.

The Colonel was waiting for us in the main hall with two of the chinas; one was serving him mate, the other offered little pastries that were a delicacy of the pampa, a kind of flower with many petals or star with many rays and candied sweet potato in the middle. Later, that self-same girl would show me how to make them. Hernández was ashen and we were extremely pale. He was embarrassed, or at least seemed to be: he didn't speak to us, he just showered insults on the chinas, damn Indians, are you trying to burn my tongue off with boiling mate and burning pastries, what are you, idiots or murderers? He didn't look at us either until Liz touched his hand, Colonel, how are you feeling this morning? We all ate far too much yesterday, and we were sick during the night too. That cheered the old guy up; he looked at her, took her hand and kissed it, and began to talk without the venom of just a moment before and without the solemnity of the previous night. You could tell he was one of those men that goes all serious with drink, because alcohol makes some people pompous, some tender, some argumentative, and they can all be the same person depending on the circumstances. I knew that only too well from my husband and his drunken antics, which would become legendary when other people started singing his songs in places where he'd never set foot, as I would discover right there in Hernández's fort. My dear girl, yes, we ate too much, but my delight in having you here is also just too much! Let's have some of my eggs, some of my bread and cheese, and let's drink some of this mate made from the restorative leaves of this fine land and then let's go out for a walk to blow away the cobwebs in the clean pampa air. Though it clearly doesn't have a salutary effect on everyone; just look at these cretins, these moronic Indians don't even know how to brew a decent mate.

The sun was still mild as we followed them out, him and the girls, one carrying hot water for the mate and the other carrying the pastries as though the food and drink were part of their bodies, or rather the other way around, the girls formed part of a single body of mate and food, a mere appendage to the needs of the Colonel. The shadows were still long and all the shades of green of the landscape and the pasture itself had the vividness of tender shoots, although little was growing any more; I felt alive, like an animal, like my Estreya, who ran towards me full of happiness at the new day which was always, for my little dog, a great feat or triumph, never something to be taken for granted. I also felt strangely alone, as if separating my body from Liz's had opened a wound: I was but a few steps away from her and yet, or maybe for that reason, seeing her so much herself, so complete without me though she wasn't going anywhere, made me ache and awakened my fears.

My love sickness was interrupted by the sight of a wall of gauchos as highly polished as British boots, sparkling clean gauchos shining like the Colonel's Bohemian crystal glasses, coiffed and elegant, clean-shaven, with their hair slicked back, I could almost swear they were wearing cologne, and dressed in brown breeches, white shirts, and black canvas slippers. Just like back in the wagon I was surprised to learn that Indians can be heroic, I was struck dumb by the gauchos, it was a kind of revelation that they could be so neat and tidy, forgetting that I myself had gone from china to lady and from lady to young gentleman. The dance that the gauchos performed to the cries of the foreman had two parts, One! Two! One! Two! like a miserable kind of music for giving orders. The gauchos, face down, each on a white sheet, raised and lowered their rigid bodies like planks, using the strength of their arms alone. Gymnastics, said Liz approvingly to the Colonel, How wonderful! You are such a modern gentleman. Press-ups is what they were doing, and they were synchronised in a way that reminded me of flocks of birds back at the settlement; some birds would weave themselves together as if they were one, one thing made of separate parts. I've liked watching birds ever since I was a girl, and I still do; they just keep on interweaving together as if nothing at all in the world has changed. Although, I wasn't so sure I liked watching those gauchos. When they were done they all stopped at once, rolled their sheets into small bundles, hung them from a loop on their belts, stood one behind the other keeping an arm's distance apart and then began jogging in a circle. This gymnastics was a kind of clumsy dance. The gauchos finally stopped, opened their legs a bit, and, keeping them straight, bent their torsos down until they could grab their feet in their hands. They did this many times until the foreman ordered them to Stand at Ease!

Good morning, my gaucho brothers! shouted the Colonel. Good morning our master and brother, God grant you a long life! answered the virile chorus of young men standing in a formation of five lines of twenty, in order of height. Time to recite some poetry, my gauchos! Yes, Sir! And standing firmly to attention, with their heads held high they chorused:

Friendship is our golden rule,
We help our friends in need.
We rescue them when life's at stake
But ne'er on them demands shall make;
A loyal friend will always take
This rule to be his creed.

Unity in brotherhood
Protects us from our foe.
Be true to all your gaucho kin
And stick with them through thick and thin
(When danger lurks, a fight within

Would brotherhood o'erthrow).

Gaucho brothers, you're my friends
And we are bound as one;
Boss and gauchos, naught divides,
Like heads and tails – one coin, two sides,
We are as one, in this take pride,
Like bullets from a gun.

Like Indian chieftains with their steeds,
Like fatherland and estate,
Just as the flower with scent is cloaked
Together our destinies are yoked
And all for one we gaucho folk
Will make our country great.

Liz jumped up and applauded, almost dancing, rippling the frills of the delicate white dress she was wearing that morning; she loved the gauchos' performance. When she got tired of clapping she sat down again and Hernández stood up, took off his hat and said Lord, we thank you for the gifts you have bestowed on us, grant us a good day's work, then he launched in with: Our Father of gauchos, who art in heaven, hallowed be thy name, thy kingdom come to this estancia, thy will be done on these fields as it is in heaven, give us this day our daily bread and forgive us our debts as we forgive our debtors and deliver us from evil, Amen.

Then the Colonel ordered Get to work, brothers! and the gauchos went off in separate groups. Hernández told us that what the gauchos had recited was just a few little verses he himself had dashed off during an unfortunate spell he'd spent holed up in a hotel on the Avenida de Mayo in Buenos Aires. One day I'd see the port city for myself with the avenue with its lights and bars, with its theatre and Spanish-style houses. So anyway, he went on, he'd written the first part of his poem about a gaucho outlaw there after coming to the realisation that gauchos were only good-for-nothing larvae because they were trapped on the estancias with no schooling, and because the city folk exploited the countryside and were even greater parasites than the gauchos themselves.

What we'd heard was from the second part of the poem, written after Hernández had restored his name to honour, and was living in Indian Territory with his own soldiers, who were learning to be farmhands and lookout men, drovers and dab hands with the bolas, sharp shooters and vets, skilled horse riders and horse breakers. It was no easy task, having to form men for this century, it was an educational undertaking that few understood. Many said there was no need to spare the blood of gauchos, but he did spare it: he considered the gauchos every bit a part of the estancia as any one of the cows and he wouldn't let a single one die without good reason. He'd even written the continuation of his poem, an instructive booklet it was, he explained, a manual for the education of agricultural labourers, so that they could truly understand that they, the farmhands and the master of the estancia, like the Colonel and his soldiers, were all one thing. And the only country they were going to get was the one they were building for the colonels and landowners, who, like him, had to learn to do everything themselves in a burgeoning nation, they were all in the same boat.

Look, look, come up here with me, my dear girl! – around midday the mate gourd was topped up with a bit of caña to whet the appetite – and Hernández began climbing up the lookout post. We all followed him even though he was only talking to Liz. Once at the top he spread his arms out in a lordly gesture, taking in the entire horizon and turning around like a fine lady dancing a minuet with dainty little steps, quite at odds with his hefty physique, and he went on: What can you see? Nothing but my own work. There are no cities, no people, no roads, no other farmers, no culture. There is nothing here, my dear. Do you really think they could build anything on their own? What did they build? Hovels, no more sophisticated than the skeletons and hides they put inside them! They are creatures of the land, my good lady, they are one and the same as the land, they are made of the same stuff as they eat, and they never emerge from the primordial mud. They need me, they need us, of course we need them too, but they can be replaced by others. No one can replace me, I have sold a million books, I have led troops into thirty-six battles, I have cultivated so many fields, hither and yon, further than you can see with those pretty little eyes of yours that don't miss a thing. Give me another mate, damn you! he barked, turning to the china, what, have you fallen asleep? Fill it right up. He sucked on the metal straw, and started climbing down again just as a couple of gauchos began to climb up, I think so that if the Colonel lost his footing they would break his fall with their own bodies.

He didn't fall on top of them. Liz looked fascinated, she was looking at him with something like love, which made it hard for me to breathe. We went for a walk, the old man taking Liz's arm and Rosa and I following a bit behind, with Rosa ranting about how he was being treated on Hernández's estancia. He too had had to wash with soap: the gauchos washed every night before eating. All the unmarried men slept in the kitchen around the fire; they wouldn't let them set up home on their own so as to avoid certain vices. What vices, Rosa? You know what I'm talking about. No, I said, What vices? Of men lying together or looking for girls and then not being fit for work because their master only wants them to work, to be clean, to learn to read, and to go to mass. Fiestas are forbidden except on Saturdays and even then he only allows them a tiny drop of caña, never mind how much he puts away himself. No one can have more than one girl. They have to get up at the bugle call, wash, get dressed, have breakfast, do their exercises and then start work at the next bugle call. They do different kinds of jobs, some that aren't even meant for gauchos: metal work, wood work, milling the grain, that's one thing, but growing flowers and fruit, baking bread, patching up shoes, sewing shirts, that's women's work, Jo, and then there's sowing corn and millet and squash and vegetables, the master makes them eat vegetables, and then they have to fight for all they've grown with the insects that devour everything, the way pumas eat hares, and on top of all that the frosts and the hail. Being a farmer is like being at war, Rosa explained to me, all the more determined in his plans to raise cattle and nothing else.

I hurried to catch up, Liz and Hernández were chatting under a red-leafed tree, sitting on a rug spread with fruit, water, cheese, bread and wine. That was called a picnic. He was explaining his plan to her: what he was creating was more than just an estancia, slowly but surely he was building a modern city, he was putting each gaucho through a process that started as soon as they arrived at the fort, until they became a part of it. The gaucho would be given the hardest tasks first, like digging the ditch that was gradually enclosing the estancia, not so much because the Colonel considered it particularly useful but because he needed something to get the new men used to hard graft, to tire them out so that at night they would collapse exhausted instead of getting drunk, and thus there would be no need to punish them – you have to have a cool head to know how to drink

– the Colonel needed to get them used to waking up and going to sleep at the same time every day, get them used to the cycles of activity and to hygiene. It was also a rite of passage, the ditch was almost a branding iron, something to mark the men; from then on a new life had begun. He made them dig a grave for their pasts, a frontier, a before and after. It was the first step in shaking them out of the larva stage. Then they would begin to help out those who were already skilled at diverse tasks. And there was the school. Those who had been there longer could now read and write. Hernández let them have the Bible because religion teaches good things like monogamy. And obedience to the Lord. And you're the Lord, aren't you? Liz asked him and the two of them laughed and the first crack appeared in my new-found faith. It didn't matter, I said to myself, trembling but also happy, if life was going to present me with more nights like the one I'd just had I wasn't going to need a god.

The nation needed the land to be conquered, Hernández went on, explaining the bones that surrounded the estancia, those savages didn't give it to us for free. And now we are conquering a workforce for the nation, just look at my gauchos. And yes, we could see them. The married ones had cottages with more than one room, the whole family can't share, said Hernández and I guess he was right. Did all of them like it? No, some needed a good hiding to see reason, others the stocks, various others needed to be whipped and some escaped never to return, fed up with being denied a daily ration of caña and their own money. Didn't he pay them? No, the little money that comes in I invest in the schoolmistress, the school, the chapel and homes for the new families. And in my cattle and my house as well, since they are the life blood of the estate, the spearhead of the nation, they are progress penetrating the desert.

A Bunch of Short Dark Hapsburgs

Hernández was showing us the man of the future, which he embodied: I am paved roads, I am steam power, I am economy of the pampas, I am seed of civilisation and progress in this fertile and brutish land, untouched by the plough, only galloped over by savages who seem to have no sense of history other than as ghosts and thieves, a mere puff of smoke with no notion of anything except sowing vandalism left right and centre; they seem to float above the ground, if it weren't for the fact that they rob and burn everything the white man's work puts in front of them, you'd think they didn't exist, that they're a folk tale like the El Dorado our ancestors went after. The gauchos, who are usually a mixture of Indian and Spaniard, didn't even inherit their European grandfathers' dreams of piles of gold. Nor did they inherit the Indians' way of going about, always treading as lightly as hares. Nothing. They were good soldiers for the nation, that's for sure, gauchos are brave, but now there aren't any wars except the ones to conquer the frontier yard by yard with the slow weapons of agricultural work. And they're just not interested. They haven't the least notion of construction, they live all hugger-mugger in mouldy hovels. They have no taboos; if they don't lie down with their mothers it's only because they prefer them young, although you can't even be sure of that, I've had three cases, no, wait a minute, Hernández consulted his ledger, four cases of men having relations with their mothers: you should see how their kids turned out, stunted, bow-legged, with skinny arms, one of them even squired son-brothers with underbites, a bunch of short dark Hapsburgs, illiterate, and toothless by the age of thirteen, that's what I get in return for giving those little brutes food, work and schooling, the Colonel exclaimed, roaring with laughter. And I had to train them using harsh methods because school or no school, you can't spare the rod. Have you seen Miss Daisy? I brought one of those gringa schoolteachers that President Sarmiento is so keen on down here to teach, and only three or four gauchos learnt anything at all, the others couldn't even write their names after a whole year. Anyway, she got raped by five of them all at once, they whipped her until one of her lovely little sky-blue eyes popped out, they knocked three of her teeth out and pulled out half her hair. I had seen her in passing, yes, a lame cross-eyed and half-bald gringa. I didn't ask about her limp, what was the point. I'd also sent those men to the other school and I have to give them credit for trying to improve the race: the little half-gringo bastards they produced turned out to be better workers; there's no point pretending otherwise, said Hernández eyeing up Liz so lecherously it was as though he had the stiff cock of a dog on either side of his nose. That gringa is tough, she was in bed for a week, and she was clever enough to insist on keeping her position as their teacher and on asking me to spare the men's lives, imagine my dear, I was in such admiration of her mercifulness. As soon as she could stand, she got up bright and early and went to where the gauchos were, the gauchos for whose lives she had wept in my arms. You can't imagine how much she had changed in just a few hours; barely overnight, where those blue eyes used to be she now had a gash on one side and a fountain of hate on the other, her remaining eye isn't even blue anymore, it turned the colour of eternal ice, it's terrifying, try and catch a glimpse when you see her. She got the men out of their cell and ordered that the five of them be stretched out between stakes on the ground. She formed a star shape with their bodies and left them to roast in the sun; hours later, maybe fourteen hours later – and this was in the height of summer – she had some buckets of water thrown over them, and as night fell she let them have some water to drink. In the sky the fluffy red clouds looked like ticks, thousands of blood-sucking ticks bunched up there against the emerging colours of orange and hot purple, and that fateful sky really should have told us what was coming but no, the gauchos asked her for forgiveness, por favor, Miss, we're sorry, we didn't mean to, it's just that you're so pretty and we'd drunk so much caña, we want to marry you, Miss, all five of us, we want to be your servants, forgive us. Miss Daisy ordered that they be given something to eat, some mush and a drop of caña, the gauchos took hope, thank you Miss, gracias, we will always be grateful to you Miss, and, feeling encouraged, they even smiled, and the Miss in question looked at them through the frozen nothingness of her empty eye and her full eye without saying anything. She sat down in the middle of the star shape made of men and asked to be brought a stout branch and a knife, and there she sat, sharpening the stick while they watched her and became less and less capable of speech, and more and more pale, more and more prone to sobbing, and their mothers and women and children gathered round to sob too, and even their horses seemed to be crying at what they had coming to them, the unleashed fury of Miss Daisy. Even I weakened slightly in my resolve to allow her to choose their punishment; there are some things you just don't do to a man, whatever the crime, but I had given my word that I would respect the fate that she had chosen for her aggressors. I thought that she would choose mercy; how wrong a man can be, even a man of my age and experience! The other gauchos looked like they would protect the men, I had to get in the middle with my shotgun and all my officers had to stand in their way, all eleven of us were armed and we had to intervene, it was the closest we have ever come to a mutiny here at Las Hortensias. What can I say? I didn't fire a single shot because the gauchos were in the right. They kept still until the gringa got tired and went back to her sick bed. Then we lowered our weapons and the gauchos went to get the bodies of the dead men, so encrusted in their own shit and dried blood that they had to be dragged out of the muck and scrubbed clean in order to be able to put them back in the ground again. If only they'd been that clean, white and cold in the first place, they'd have avoided ending their days as dirty, hot-blooded darkies. I myself wept that night.

Liz nodded while he spoke, from time to time she would rest her hand on his shoulder, she called him a hero and said you're a true patriot, and she kept filling his glass because if the Colonel had pricks where other people have eyes, he also had ten thirsty camels where other people have mouths, his mouth was basically an end point, a pool of whisky where all his pricks drowned. Well handled! said Liz. She had Hernández wrapped around her little finger. What have you done with the degenerates and their mothers? she asked him. I am forcing them to learn in the tough part of the school, which I was telling you about, where we beat it into them, Miss Daisy's school. She runs both schools but I have a feeling that the fear she inspires in them means those darkies will never learn anything, ever. And where is the other school? Over there behind those trees, Hernández said, pointing to a flat patch of ground cleared of scrub. He called out and one of his clean and coiffed gauchos appeared. Hernández ordered him to escort the ladies, which made the gaucho snigger. Hernández sniggered too at which point I drew my knife and he said to me no, no my lad, no offence, I'm not calling you a señora; what I meant was your sister is lady enough for two, and he sent us to visit the school for disobedient gauchos.

The blonde woman and her bastard twins were in charge there. The boys had turned out fierce and quite white and it was exactly for that reason – because nothing was right unless it was like their mother – that they hated gauchos. They imagined what they could have been if it hadn't been for those five men killed in a bloody and shit-filled star. They wanted to go back to the United States with their mother and be cowboys in Minneapolis. Let's go back home, momma they would say to her, as if there was any *back* for them to go to beyond Hernández's estancia.

The Whip and the Rod

No door was closed to us. Hernández showed us everything with patrician pride. Stiff and drying out like hides in the sun, skin cracked, eyes shut, faces contorted in pain: that's how we found the gauchos in Campo Malo, the place that Hernández kept for outcasts. Being sentenced to death was primarily for deserters and murderers, the worst crimes that could be committed at Las Hortensias. Everything else, including stealing, was considered a minor offence, punishable by spread-eagling between four stakes, by the stocks, or by whipping with knotted, wetted reins. What you couldn't do was leave. Or kill. The death sentence that awaited murderers was to be put inside the hide of a freshly slaughtered cow, a method they called the beef roll. The poor wretch would be rolled in the cow's skin, stitched inside it and left outside in the blazing sun: slowly the hide would tighten, smothering him as it dried, hour after hour, until he was dead.

After being punished – unless the punishment was death – each gaucho was squeezed into a small space containing only hides and dirt then bound hand and foot, like cattle snagged with bolas, so that the damned idlers couldn't just lie down to sleep. The Little Daisies explained their methods to us, they were only about fifteen, but every bit as tough as their momma: they would cover the men's eyes with blinkers and gag them with bridles, then throw them to the ground, and lash their bodies with whips. The men were bloodied bundles, speckled black and blue from all the flies they couldn't swat, and they were kept like that because they do not want to learn. They were kept in punishment boxes after their day in the stocks, or the stakes, and were left to do a week of penance so that they would be reformed. Then they were allowed to go, and off they went, like this stupid nigger, for example – the taller of Miss Daisy's offspring kicked the skinned head of a gaucho on flesh so raw it hurt to see it – who ran off to his mother's house, so that he could suck the tits of that whore of a witch who was his mother and wife in the same body. And we had others, a couple of them managed to escape from us, like that bone-idle man who sang instead of working, and who learnt his letters so he could write down his songs and then went around saying that the bossman had stolen his poems and we gave him a taste of the whip and the rod and then we gave him a bit more and he wouldn't stop saying that the songs were his, and we had him ready to be broken in, you know ma'am, a horse in front to pull him one way and a horse behind for the other way, and we were going to have one horse run towards Great Britain and one towards Indian Territory, but that scumbag larva escaped. We knew he was a worm because he wriggled free somehow. It doesn't really matter if we find him or not, what do we care about that Indian piece of shit and all these damn Indians? they said, spitting on the men, and there was something so menacing about them, they were so full of themselves, so proud of what they were showing us, whereas I just wanted to get out of there, to get out of earshot of the pleas for mercy uttered by the weak voices of the dying men. Liz congratulated the boys, she told them that if she was their mother she would be so proud of them, what good boys, muy bien, hardworking and with such lovely English manners. The Little Daisies were thrilled; they stopped hitting and swearing for a while and they saw us to the door of Campo Malo.

On the rest of the estancia – the Campo Bueno was it called? – work seemed to bring happiness to everyone. The world is like a woven cloth, Liz began, what is brilliant here is like a weave that only shines because it has a warp of flesh and blood, which is Campo Malo, and that's the way it's always been, and that's the way it will remain until we all know our place in the weaving process. In this particular pattern, the gauchos and the chinas – who didn't do gymnastics because at that time of the morning they were giving breakfast to their children – worked with dedication from eight in the morning until eight at night. They would sing 'See our beloved flag that waves/its emblem is our beacon/Oh Argentina fought so braaaaave/to give us all our freedom!' and would do their work by parts. What I mean is that no one did a whole job, no one finished what they started. The washerwomen, for example, sat at the sides of huge basins, the first ones soaked and soaped the clothes. They would pass them down the line to the next group of women who would scrub them with brushes. They in turn would pass them along to be rinsed. And finally the white shirts, shining like the sun, would be hung out to dry by dark-skinned women. It was the same at the furnace: one man would stoke the fire, another would heat the metal until it was soft enough, one would hammer it into the desired shape and plunge it into cold water and another would take it out all sleek and shiny and put it up on a stand. In just one day I saw hundreds of horseshoes being made using this formula: the Colonel wanted to invent a new speed on the pampa, he'd been to Great Britain and the United

States of America and he wanted for the Argentines something of the forceful zeal of the Anglos. Only men worked in the furnace and, when the foreman was out of earshot, these men sang songs as they stared at the chinas: 'A cap the girl frog was a'knitting/to give to a boy frog one day/Well mind how you go little girl frog/For this frog needs a roll in the hay'.

The Colonel held another huge dinner that night and ended up blind drunk on wine again. The patriarch's head hadn't even hit the table before Liz sprang from her chair and led me, practically shoving me, to her bed. It wasn't that I minded, I was merely trying to ask, trying to understand why she was acting so queer with me, she had been so different during our journey. But you like it, don't you? she interrupted, giving me one last shove. I fell onto the bed with a bounce and she rushed to get my clothes off like she was rushing to put out a fire. She took her clothes off as well and continued with my education: this time she began gently, stroking my whole body, front and back, with her hands, her mouth, her tongue, her nose and she even stuck her nipples into all my holes. I was lost for words, even though this woman had taught me so many of them as we crossed the desert, inside the wagon, by the fire, under the ombú trees, and drinking caña with Rosa. The chinas knocked at the door and came in, I hid while they filled the tub with hot water, Liz asked them to bring some tea, which they did, and then they went away. She grabbed me all over again and stuck me in the bath and got in herself, and then she did something no one had ever done to me: she turned me round, sinking her breasts onto my shoulder blades, biting me hard on the back of my neck like a dog carrying its pup across a river, she never once let go of me, with one hand she began to rub my nipples and with the other my cunt, she parted my buttocks, and leaning there, she grabbed my hand and taught me to touch myself, she sucked my fingers, she put them on my clitoris, using my hand as if it were hers until I found my own rhythm, she opened my arse a bit more and then penetrated me with her fist while she bit me harder and harder and kept squeezing my breasts. I stopped touching myself, I grabbed the sides of the tub with both hands and allowed myself to be filled up with this new pleasure, almost stinging, a pleasure made of needles and pins, she made me howl like an animal in her arms. I came in my arse, pledged her eternal love, and then sucked her till I nearly drowned.

That Strange Gaucho Who
Fancied Himself as a Writer

Oh, do tell us about that strange gaucho who fancied himself as a writer! The one who ran away, Liz launched straight in over breakfast, right after the formal good mornings, which were becoming less and less formal, to my delight and alarm: even before the first rays of sun came into the bedroom I'd woken up practically drowning with Liz's cunt in my mouth and her rubbing herself against my face, my breathing syncopated with her secretions, she made me breathe in and out to her rhythm as if she were breaking me in. That was what she was doing whether I realised it or not, how better to tame an animal than by forcing it to breathe when you choose? Now she was kissing the Colonel on the cheek. He always looked grey in the mornings but nevertheless he was up and about at the crack of dawn. Hernández was a tamer too, a tamer of hangovers who could even muster a smile when she looked at him or addressed him in any way. Do you see, darling? There are sparks of genius here in the countryside, as I always say when people ask me what the folk on the pampas are like. A semi-illiterate gaucho learnt something here with Miss Daisy, and now he says I stole his songs. Oh, yes, quite an odd fellow, by the sound of it? Yes, yes, though he does have a point: I didn't steal them, but when I heard him sing I relieved him of his ploughing duties so that he could entertain the men while they worked. What a generous man you are, Colonel! If you say so, my little Gringa, then I must be. The truth is, I realised that it made them happier, and a leader, a Colonel like myself, a landowner, has to know how to handle his troops and keep them happy. It has to be carrot and stick, especially when there are a thousand of them and only twenty-one of us military men, me and my officers; if I count the gauchos who believe in progress, there are two hundred of us. I'd rather not be put in the position of having to test their loyalty, just in case I've backed the wrong horse and they decide to bolt. I have to stable them, do you see? I have to make them feel they belong here, that it's their home territory. And it is partly theirs: the land a man works is always partly his. Not always. I said partly, my dear, don't worry, I haven't been bitten by the communist bug, the plague that all these starving peasants are trying to bring over from Europe like a swarm of locusts, just as our grandfathers flattened us with their smallpox; I have to laugh, Gringa, everything is so flat here, they paved the way. Just imagine, darling, one day the gauchos will realise that they far outnumber us, and although they know — because they do know, they're not completely daft and some of them have been around a fair bit — that the Argentine Army is behind us, and therefore also partly behind them but mainly behind us — here we're all in it together but not to the same extent, some of us are completely in it and others only partly, perhaps I'm not being clear — as I say, one day they'll realise, and then before the first battalion can arrive, they'll already have slit our throats, as they are so fond of doing when they get the chance — you should hear them sing along while a dying man pirouettes in a pool of his own blood! So the long and short of it is, I gave the gaucho writer a job as a performer and sometimes I'd listen to that brute singing and you should have heard the lines he came up with. That ruffian was actually, how shall I put it, a real poet of the people. I did stick a few lines of his poetry into my first book; he wasn't totally wrong about that. I also put his name in the title, Martín Fierro is the name of that peasant poet, who's capable of churning out rhymes all day long, it's practically a kind of vice with him, though he's good at it. He never appreciated what I did for him by taking some of his songs and putting them in my book. I took his voice, the voice of the voiceless, do you see, to the whole country, to the big smoke Buenos Aires which is always ripping us off. The city sponges off us, charging us huge amounts for exporting grain and cattle through its port. And not letting us build another big port anywhere else.

Hernández carried on with his monologue about the port, taxes, theft, and 'us' – by which he meant ranch owners and gauchos all lumped together because they shared the same soil and the same pressure from Buenos Aires and the war against the Indians. 'We can't be us without others', he said at one point, and I was tempted to get my notebook out and jot it down. The Colonel was no fool; I felt I was learning like I had in the wagon with Liz, as though bandages were being lifted from my eyes. I felt I had as many layers over my eyes as an Egyptian mummy, those bodies wrapped in strips of cloth and laid in pyramids, gigantic tombs made thousands of years ago in the sands of the north of Africa, that continent of giraffes and elephants. I was also itching to whack him on the head with a stick and run away somewhere, anywhere. I recognised the lines of poetry; it was my husband who'd written them and if they were his property, then Hernández had also stolen from me. And from my children. That morning, sitting beside the landowner, although I was dressed as Liz's brother Joseph Scott, I was actually a wife who'd been cheated; I realised the Colonel had robbed me of something that was mine and should rightfully belong to my children. For the first time in my life I felt that I was the owner of something; on the estancia I could see how nice it was to own things, and I felt indignant. I decided then and there that I wouldn't leave the fort empty-handed: justice would be done. And also knowing that Fierro was near, that I was following his path, made me worry about coming across him and being sent back to where I'd come from, back beside him in our shack. Surely it wouldn't come to that? The brute had run away, he was a deserter now, he couldn't come back to the estancia, but what if he tried to drag me away? Hearing his name had made me determined to keep dressing as a man and never let my shotgun out of my sight. Suddenly it all became clear to me: the books containing Fierro's poetry were selling like hot cakes, and it was my money, but there was no way I was going back to our old shack. And certainly not with Fierro. The old Colonel was still going on about port tariffs and the common good and the great dilemma facing Argentina. How can a country grow if those who make it prosper are robbed and penalised? Hernández went on. I found my own thoughts wandering back and forth. Who makes Argentina grow? I wondered. What are taxes and what's the point of them? The old man still hadn't shut up; he went back to the subject of Fierro, recounting that they called him the Cock for a time until (and Hernández chuckled at this point) they discovered his vices and had to change his nickname pronto. Liz, do you know what they started calling him? Excuse me for saying it, I don't want to be rude, but it's the truth and no amount of pussyfooting around will change it. The truth is neither pretty nor ugly, good or bad, fat or thin, federal or unitarian, country or city: it's just the truth, wouldn't you agree? Well, so, the truth is that the Cock turned out to be more of a Hen and that's what they started calling him round here. Not because he was a coward, he always had his knife at the ready, if he could, the gaucho singer would have spent his whole time fighting people, but because he was a, how should I put it, the word here is bufarrón, would it be poof in English? He was spotted canoodling with another gaucho. I had both of them staked out in Campo Malo but I wasn't born yesterday: no amount of staking out will straighten something so bent.

Liz and the Colonel had me totally in their sway: first I had to breathe to the rhythm of her passion, as she alternately filled and emptied my mouth in her undulating dance. Then, depending on what Hernández was saying, I was either heading back to the old shack or towards a bag of money. I wasn't sure if what the Colonel said was true, I'd had Fierro on top of me enough times to know that he wasn't as bent as all that. When you stopped to think, he'd had it off with me and, only a matter of hours ago, I'd been under a cunt that, if it felt so inclined, could have suffocated me. These new inclinations that the father of my children and I had each developed put a huge distance between myself and the shack. I must have breathed a big sigh of relief because Hernández looked at me and laughed. Don't worry, my boy, it's not catching, you'll soon see a bit more of the world and nothing people do in bed will surprise you. Excuse me Madam for putting it so bluntly, you're a married woman, you're not easily shocked, are you? Liz blushed and the Colonel, who was adding neat caña to the mate the chinas had brought him, started apologising; but before he could finish, Liz stormed out. He remained silent for a while, sucking at his mate, with a vacant expression. Just look at her, my little gringo friend. Sorry, I know she's your sister, but she goes around showing me her udders all day long and then runs off blushing at the slightest bit of fun! Women are like horses, my lad: you have to whip them till they realise they like being dominated, do you see? You'll soon get the hang of it. You can start right here if you haven't already, I've got a few little chinas who are as tasty as a freshly baked bun, young things. I don't break them all in, just a few; I'm getting on a bit now and have to be a bit more picky about which ones I go for. He went on in this vein for hours without my having to say anything except to mutter in agreement from time to time, just to reassure him that he wasn't talking to himself.

Punch and Whisky

Offended, or feigning offence, I wasn't quite sure which, Liz gave the Colonel a wide berth all day, leaving him shipwrecked in his sea of drink, while he stammered out apologies. I beg your pardon, lo siento mucho, my dear, one does become rather rough and ready living amongst these brutes, there's no getting away from it, he apologised, every time he saw her going past with one of his officers, who in turn tried to keep away from her for fear of the punishment they'd receive if the Colonel felt slighted. It was like that the whole day: her running away from him, them avoiding her, and me watching it all without really understanding, stuck there beside the old man, who grabbed my arm every time I made as if to leave. At some point Liz relented. I don't know whether she felt sorry for me or for him, but we were both relieved. She came over to us and said to the old man that she was arranging a surprise for him with the officers. What did you say? he almost shouted. An English dinner, you will love it. Whatever it is, I will love it as long as you are here, he responded gallantly, trying to get up and bow to her, but instead he fell headlong onto the ground, like a duck diving into water when it spots a fish. Oh, Colonel, caña is a terribly cheap drink, let me help you up. Yes, you're right. By all means, do help me up, he said while a couple of gauchos were already carrying him into the house. Water and a lie-down, Liz ordered the chinas, who ran to his room ahead of the Colonel, who by then had passed out and was being carried over the shoulder of one of his men.

Liz took charge of the kitchen: there she was, with that radiance of hers, that ghostly whiteness and the red of coloured maize, and she was so indifferent towards me that I clung to her side, trying to overcome the need to bury myself in her skin, to remain on the warm island of her voice. But I couldn't. We were leaving soon, and she told me to discreetly get our things prepared, as she brought a barrel of whisky and jars of curry in from the wagon. So I got ready, together with Rosa and Estreya, who was following us everywhere fearfully; he'd been forced to sleep outdoors with the other dogs and had been nipped a fair few times, poor thing. The Colonel had a specific place for everyone and there was no way a dog would be allowed inside his house. When I'd finished my tasks and while the Colonel was otherwise engaged I let Estreya into the kitchen, and made a fuss of him while he whimpered, as if talking to me and telling me all the awful things that had happened. I calmed him down, stroking him and feeding him scraps of meat. I promised I'd never let anything like that happen to him again, that from now on he'd always sleep with me. Right then and there he went to sleep, lying on his back, surrendering his exposed neck to me, trusting me, and Liz looked fondly at us for a while before getting me to help again. I had to peel and chop oranges and lemons, the only fruit that they had there at Las Hortensias, until my arms were nearly dropping off. She was making punch: they had brought her the huge army pots and pans, so big you could have boiled a man alive standing up in each of them. Caña and fruit, four pots for the gauchos, two others with whisky and fruit, and a lamb curry with carrot and squash for the officers, that was what Liz had made. She was sure she'd be able to persuade the Colonel to let the workers have a drink too.

And so she did. She put on a blue dress and let her hair down: she was a vision. The old man must have thought so too when she went to his room to ply him with coffee, water and whisky. She made him drink the jug of freshly drawn water, gave him his coffee, chatted inconsequentially and made him promise he'd never drink caña again. He swore he never would, doubtless tickled that she should care about his state of health. Finally she gave him a glass of her good Scotch whisky and the Colonel was himself once more, feeling forgiven in exchange for allowing everyone to come to the party. She emerged looking radiant and ordered the servants to lay the table with a cloth and candles, crystal glasses in the dining room and the kitchen, and then the gauchos struck up their guitars: Fierro wasn't the only one with a ditty to sing. The workers spruced themselves up as if they were going to a palace; they'd never drunk from Bohemian crystal glasses before, they'd never tasted punch, they washed, brushed and shaved themselves, plaited their hair and shined their shoes until they looked more like English boots than gaucho boots with hooves for heels. The soldiers smoothed down their uniforms and pinned on their medals, wearing cologne and sporting burnished swords. It was like Christmas at the estancia when the owners are in residence, there was a party atmosphere, that feeling of happiness that times of plenty bring to almost everyone, especially to those for whom it's rare. Ten whole calves were splayed over the gauchos' fire, the curry for the officers was beginning to give off a good smell, and the gauchos and their chinas set to dancing as soon as the punch was served; they called Liz's drink puncho, on the basis that every gaucho needs his poncho, so every gaucho should partake of the puncho. They enjoyed it so much that they wouldn't let go of their glasses until well into the morning.

Liz had a very simple plan, but she hadn't told me it beforehand because she was convinced that I was hopeless at keeping a secret: the three of us were going to leave as we had arrived, but we were not going to leave on our own. We were going to take the gauchos who were most skilled at tracking with us, and those who knew the meaning of hard work. To set up our estancia we would need blacksmiths, flower-growers, people who knew how to distil whisky and how to build a stone house, how to get cows to yield their best milk and how to coax strawberries to grow, even in the desert. Rosa had sized the gauchos up and Liz had inspected their work. When we arrived there were three of us and we were going to leave with twenty more, the workers would go first and we'd follow on behind. Justice would be done. I found out the whole plan that afternoon, before the party began, and it made me so happy that I was just as merry as the rest of them, who were gradually losing themselves in a state of total drunkenness. The workers stamped their feet, and it was quite a sight, their gaucho boots raised a cloud of dust which the girls with their skirts whirled around like a hurricane. Even the children danced, the kitchen became a dance floor and gradually officers began migrating from the Colonel's room, likely bored of endless sermons on industry by the high priest of civilisation, and began mingling with the gauchos. The social boundaries between educated people and peasants, uniformed men and chinas, workers and soldiers gradually dissolved with every passing glass. Rosa wandered around outside the house, wetting the whistle of those standing guard, just a drop to let you see how good the punch is, and there the soldiers were, dropping from the watchtowers like ripe fruit from trees.

They'd begun drinking the punch at sundown. By midnight the whole house was jumping in a cloud of dust kicked up by the dancers. A few hours before sunrise, the cloud was still there: but now it was raised by the furious fornicating of chinas, gauchos and soldiers. I recall seeing a china with one gaucho in front kissing her and putting his hand up her skirt and a soldier groping her tits from behind while she had her hands full, a stiff cock in each, meanwhile, watching them, was a bandy-legged gaucho pleasuring himself, a china rubbing her tits against his back, and a swarthy, stumpy little man was resting his prick on the china's thighs while another woman was sucking his balls while another man was sucking her cunt while another woman was licking her tits while all of them carried on downing the punch and groaning, coming all over each other, like candles melting away together, until it was almost impossible to tell who was doing what with whom. They were one big writhing mass, smothered in their own stew of spunk and china juice and, before long, copious quantities of vomit; they all ended up passing out around dawn, floating in a lake surrounded by the bits of beef and oranges they'd previously eaten. Only Liz and Hernández were left in the dining room, him spread-eagled on the floor and her rearranging her dress. The end of the orgy was revolting, but we had to lie on the floor as well and get spattered with the landowner's vomit. Our twenty gauchos had left hours earlier, each riding one of Hernández's finest horses and carrying the few coins they'd managed to scrape together from their long overdue wages.

You Fucking Whore!

The scene gradually dissolved as, one by one, soldiers, workers and the Colonel began waking up. They slowly emerged from their colossal hangover, breaking the spell that had brought them together hours before. A few slipped and fell, and had to get up again. They clutched their heads, groaning; Hernández barely opened one eye before returning to the ashen grey faint in which he lay. Liz brought him water and dabbed at his face, Oh, Colonel, what a party we had! Come on, let's go to your room, you need to sleep in a bed, come on, come along Colonel, I'll look after you.

You fucking whore! You damn china! Shouts began to be heard, as the first few men surfaced and began to see who their wives had passed out with, on, beneath or beside. The men shouted more than the chinas did, but there was also the odd cry of shut up you faggot! I saw what you were up to last night. Or, fucking bitch, you stole my man! There were so many broken couples that day at Las Hortensias, so many little children crying to be fed because no one made any breakfast, so many dogs cowering with their tails between their legs. Then came the fisticuffs and ranting, men settled ownership of the women with knives and blows and the chinas fought over their men using their bare hands, and everyone shouted at the top of their voices. Another battle commenced: another chaos of bodies. Several pints of blood, five severed fingers and three bodies stabbed to death all fell to the filthy floor. It stopped there because one of the officers managed to drag himself to the gun room and fire a shot into the air. After the bang, a sad silence descended on the estancia. Nobody could do anything except vomit, ask each other for forgiveness, and cry the day away. Liz, Rosa and I did the same, although knowing we were going to leave the next day cheered us up. We were fed up with so much pretence, having so many people around, we wanted to get back to the little world of our wagon, to the vast limpid pampas, to our cows and the creatures who crawled out of the earth at night. I also felt a curious new happiness in my body: I had kissed a few girls and the gaucho they'd called a faggot. I was definitely getting a taste for them, kisses from girls and gay gauchos. I took it all in my stride. Liz was there and I wanted to spend my whole life with her, and at that point I couldn't imagine having love and freedom at the same time. But my body felt happy, something in me was giving way and it was like diving into the river on one of those hot summer days that in the pampas are so hot the air boils: it's not just a figure of speech, the scorching air quivers in the sun, distorting how you see things.

Liz looked after the old man as if he were her father. She had the armchair brought close to him and there she sat, passing him the bucket every time the poor man was about to be sick and feeding him tiny spoonfuls of tea with whisky, because there's nothing better than a hair of the dog. While she tended to him she was in tears, and made sure he noticed it; but she never answered when he asked why she was crying. The most important thing is for you to get well again, Colonel, she repeated like a litany, muttering under her breath something about being a decent married woman, about dishonouring her husband and missing him terribly.

That night, after having watched the poor chinas dragging themselves around the kitchen attempting to clean up the mess, I curled up beside Estreya. The soldiers buried the dead bodies, wondering how to punish those responsible, and took away Miss Daisy and the Little Daisies who were also feeling so rough that they weren't in a fit state to mete out punishment. The men who had killed slept off their hangovers in the cells that night, fearing what would happen when the Colonel woke up, but not fearing it as much as the officers did when they discovered that there were horses, men and women missing. A search party was sent out to look for them, but I suspect that rather than searching, all they did was lie down to sleep a few miles from the house, leaving their horses standing guard, because they found no sign of the runaways.

A sign came the next morning, when the old man was starting the day drinking tea with lemon and a few drops of whisky; at Liz's suggestion he was keeping off the mate. Hernández only found out what had happened when a lone chestnut horse arrived back at the ranch bathed in sweat, and the news hit him like the branch of an ombú falling on his head: deserters, stolen horses, dead men, and those who'd killed them awaiting their fate in their cells of earth and cowhide. He was dumbstruck. Then he began shouting and swearing. He court-martialled the officers who'd been on guard the night of the party, ordered the killers to be executed, flung the teapot and the entire tea service across the room, and only began to calm down a bit when he saw Liz crying. Please forgive me, Colonel, it's my fault, I should never have had the party, she said, her whole body shaking. In her country people could take their drink and still behave themselves, she didn't know how things were in Argentina, but please don't let anyone else be killed. The old man relented a bit, and gave all those he held responsible a week of staking out at Campo Malo. They were also demoted, lost all wages owing to them, as well as forfeiting their wages for the next two years. And they would be put to work in the ditch again. And let God decide who survives, Gringa, they'll owe you and Him their lives. As the Little Daisies also ended up staked out, Liz was reassured that the chinas would find a way to bring water and shade to their menfolk.

Goodbye, Colonel

Hernández's rage did not abate until nightfall when the whisky brought him back to his talk of rural industry, to the iron railways that would link the pampas to the port and the port with the world and with Great Britain, to the concert of nations in which Argentina would be called upon to play its part in ending hunger across the world, to his talk of educating gauchos. Look at the nonsense they get up to, Gringa! After so many years of schooling, too! Liz asked him what he thought had happened to her husband. He assured her that the Argentine Army would not detain a British subject, they will definitely have freed him, unless he's done something really bad. How dare you! Liz leapt to her feet. No, no, I'm not saying your husband is an outlaw, I'm just explaining Argentine laws to you, that's all. He'd heard of a British man who had been picked up by the law by mistake; that was a while ago, and it was also a while ago that they let him go. Show me that map again, I want to see where your land is. He looked at the map for a bit: look Gringa, I don't know who sold that land to your husband's employer, but it's still under Indian control. If he went that way the Indians must have him. Don't be frightened, they're not all that bad. Don't you lie to me, I've been reading your book. Not that bad? You're lying Colonel, I don't believe

you! You yourself recounted what they did to that poor
white woman they held captive:

> One squaw there was who hated her
> And wished she'd go to hell.
> Well, one day that squaw's sister died,
> And − seeing the pale-face close beside −
> The squaw screamed out: 'I'll have your hide!
> You killed her with a spell!'

> An Indian brave then dragged her out
> And threatened her full sore;
> Said she her witchcraft must declare,
> She must confess it, then and there,
> If she refused, revenge he'd swear
> Until she lived no more.

> The poor white woman wept and cried
> But it was all in vain,
> The Indian brave, with fury wild
> Hit out at her and seized her child,
> And with his whip he her reviled
> Till she screamed out in pain.

> That savage man, so cruel was he
> He whipped her hard and long.
> The blows fell fast, and still they fell −
> His face with furious rage did swell
> She felt the pain of death and hell,
> Though she had done no wrong.

> At last in fury he cried out
> 'For this you're going to pay!
> You killed our girl with your evil eye
> So for your son the end is nigh!'

At his cruel knife the boy did die:
Cold at her feet he lay.

Liz's reading gave Hernández his colour and his good humour back. Her accent reading the lines in Spanish seemed to amuse him, as it amused me, because he roared and roared and even cried with laughter. My darling Gringa, do you believe everything you read? I invented all that, well nearly all of it. Yes, women are taken captive and no, they aren't treated like royalty, but it's not really any worse than the way we treat the chinas. Oh, I'm so sorry Liz, I can't stop laughing, I said that they capture women but I've never heard of them slaughtering white children like lambs, and besides, some of the women seem to have quite a good time with the Indians. My mother told me about one, a British woman like yourself, who fell in love with her Indian captor and didn't want to go back to civilisation. My mother offered to take her in and get her children back, though I don't know how she would have gone about doing that, but anyway she didn't have to, as the British woman said no, she was happy living in Indian Territory with her Chief. My mother saw the blonde-haired Indian again when she went along to the general store to buy provisions and a few luxuries; they'd just slaughtered a sheep, and the Englishwoman actually jumped down from her horse to have a suck at the warm blood. Are you telling the truth now? Yes, yes, I'm not spinning you a tale. I'm just telling you what my mother told me, Gringa. I think she jumped off her horse so that my mother would see her and understand. Understand what? That she'd embraced another way of life, like you are doing here; you left Great Britain with its machines, manners and civilisation, the highest form of civilisation in the world, to come and seek your fortune on an estancia. And I don't know who can have sold that land to your employer, my dear, but I can tell you that it's not going to be easy for you to make a go of it there. Unless you do business with the Indians. But why did you lie about them? I've already told you, Liz: Argentina needs that land in order to progress. And as for the gauchos, they need an enemy to turn them into patriotic Argentines. We all need the Indians. I am creating a nation on land, in combat, and on paper, do you see? And you are helping us build that nation too. I'm not going to let you go unarmed, I'm going to give you rifles and gunpowder. And a few trinkets that Indians like. The caña that no one here will ever drink again, for a start. Tobacco. And little mirrors, the Indians are terribly vain, you'll see. Now come with me, I've got a surprise for you.

Off they went. It wasn't a night for taking risks so I went to sleep in the room that had been assigned to me. I managed to sneak Estreya in and he kept still and stayed quiet as if he understood the situation. He probably did understand a bit; outside, the fierce dogs of the gauchos would have given him a hard time again. I hugged him close and fell asleep. I would see Liz just after dawn, dressed in her wagon gear once more. She showered me in kisses and showed me the surprise that Hernández had given her: it was the diamond. He had put it on her right hand. It lent her red and white colouring even more sparkle.

PART THREE

INDIAN TERRITORY

Frothing like Foam

The grass was waving as we set off and the pampa was a two-coloured sea: when the stalks surrendered to the wind the pampa whitened, frothing like foam; when they swayed back it was green and the different shades of grass sparkled, looking like young shoots though it was too late in the year for that. Everything was returning to the earth now, going from light green, yellow, gold, and ochre to brown, and then pitching over. We were able to breathe again, as if we'd just emerged from a cave, as if the air on the estancia had been thick and foul. The air in Las Hortensias you could see through, but it was different, it was like inhaling water, it made you choke and splutter. It was suffocating: hard to breathe in or out. It must have been because of Campo Malo, the sound of the gauchos groaning as they were punished, or the repressed desires of the others for all the things they'd been denied. Yes, freedom is the best air, my darling. That's how we all felt; even the poor old oxen felt refreshed, lowering their curly eyelashes from the love they felt when we yoked them to the wagon. Estreya ran here and there, happy as any puppy, even though he was quite big, the calves were shaking hips they didn't even have in a dance that ended with them butting heads and then running towards each other again; it looked to me like they were laughing silently in that playful way that animals have of expressing their happiness. Our belly laughs spilled over onto all the animals around the wagon. Rosa was out in front, in his gaucho garb now, proud of his new horse which was a splendid chestnut, one of the four the Colonel had given us. He galloped back to us and said chuckling, Hey, look at that blue bird gringas, there's an ombú full of birds' nests, look at the cows following us like ducklings waddling after their mother, wasn't the Colonel horrible, not even letting you have a drink in peace, and not letting you gallop when you felt like it. Then he shouted Giddy up, Cielo old girl! to his horse whose leg was pawing at the dirt like a black hoe, and the sparkles from the diamond on Liz's hand galloped too, those sparkles that against her white skin and red hair left me almost blind with the desire to have her on top of me. Or underneath me. Or alongside. I'd have to wait: I was guessing that Liz wouldn't like me to touch her in front of anyone else. We ate some jerky and chutney washed down with a few glasses of the wine that Hernández had also given us. The old guy was a pest but he'd been generous with us. I felt a little twinge inside of me, I was torn between gratitude – for the four poster bed, for the chance he'd given Liz to put on those frocks she'd then enjoyed taking off with me – and feeling giddy with relief. It was as if I, having just crossed the bridge over the ditch back into the pampa, was one of those pale wispy clumps that appear on thistles after the withering of the seed-filled flowers. Flowers of a purple so vivid that it seems stolen from the sky at sunup or sundown. That's still the way I say it, even though I now know that the sun doesn't go up and down. It just goes around and around, burning itself out like any fire.

As If the Milky Way Began or
Ended Right There in Her Hands

We would arrive at the Indian encampment armed with transparency: caña, mirrors — because reflections are diaphanous too — and, best of all, Liz's shimmering diamond. I couldn't tell whether the Milky Way began or ended right there in her hands, the pampa sky unfurled from her middle finger like a river where the constellations sparkled quietly like calm stones belying their true nature as bubbling and boiling volcanoes. Liz was going over her last conversation with Hernández. 'They're not stupid, Gringa. They'll know how much that diamond is worth. But they just can't help themselves when it comes to shiny trinkets and strong drink.' 'I can understand that, Colonel, can't you?' 'A bit, yes, I can, we're only human, although some of us are impregnated with the future, destined to spill our seeds of tomorrow on virgin lands, whilst others live outside time, Gringa, like animals.' 'I suppose you're right. They'll probably like whisky too.' She was dressed in her wagon clothes again, mostly grey, dull green or brown, always modest. Liz was speaking to me as though all those nights we'd spent together had never happened, as if she'd never mixed her saliva with mine, as if, in short, there was nothing between us. The blue sky quickly covered over with looming expressive clouds: they spoke of the West, of the sun that embraced us once more despite the punishing wind, they spoke of sudden showers, the smell of rain carried on the wind, of the earth breathless and ready to receive the rain, they spoke of my desire for the sky to come tumbling down so that we'd have to stop and Liz and I would have to get back inside the wagon, so I'd have to strip off the sodden clothing stuck to her body, after seeing her dash to put up the lightning rod and after I'd run about rounding up the hens. They were clucking and fussing that day as they always did when there was a storm, but even more nervously this time, it must have been the flash of lightning which bounced off Liz's ring, dazzling them, that made them lay the sparkling eggs that would later hatch into the glossy black-plumed cockerels that Kaukalitrán would adore.

As silky and glossy blue-black as their feathers was that night; our night.

The Earth Croaked

When the rain had passed the earth croaked, birds splashed in the puddles, flapping their wings and setting the air chirping, and the rainbow had one leg shorter than the other: since leaving the estancia the world had started to slope upwards. I'd only just noticed it, blinded as I was by the need to touch Liz, for her to touch me, as if bread and water sprang from her hand, the air I needed to stay alive even. With Liz, everything had become the pain of choking desire, the tension of the thread that bound us, whilst I was cut up imagining our separation as soon as we found Oscar. But I'd never seen a lame rainbow, nor had I seen the earth curve upwards leaving the pastures down yonder, pastures that spread out with the soft grace of ruffles on a dress, waves of violet and yellow flowers each with their diminutive shadows; because shadows were falling everywhere, adorning everything with subtle contrasts, and higher up and further on, the herons and biguás and flamingos heralded a lagoon. Everything that morning, life itself, was a warm embrace.

What goes up must come down, even the planet; I'd just learnt that and now the poor oxen were learning it. Even going downhill they had no respite; rather than pulling, they had to brace themselves, and they tried to look behind to see what was pushing them. I think they already felt like the wagon was part of them, so they must have thought a part of themselves was bearing down on them; they wanted to escape, on they trotted until tufts of waving reeds began to appear on either side of the Indian trail. We stopped and unyoked them; Rosa got an asado going, partly because he was hungry and partly because the mosquitoes and black barigüí flies were eating us alive and the smoke would repel them. There was no other sign of life until Rosa caught three cuys and the little critters began to scream, their little paws scratching at this giant man, their bodies arched in pain; we were their Campo Malo, poor things. Then, a little while later, the smell of their flesh browning in the fire wafted over, and we were satisfied body and soul.

An Erratic Flight

Like the sense of peace rising from our full bellies, mushrooms sprang up from the damp earth. The pampas carried on undulating gently and I realised that undulations appear to sway even though they are still, and that they have more colours than the plain: like a dog stretching, the whole earth arched its back and the stiff fur of its uneven hillocks looked like water with reflections rippled by the wind. Where once life on the road had seemed sky-blue to me, now it went from deep purple to lilac, to yellow and orange, to white, to light green and dark green, occasionally allowing a rare glimpse of brown. It was as though the rainbow's shorter leg had spread its colours on the ground, and so it went on, getting stronger and more clearly defined, as if the colours found their true nature as we went along, and the earth itself took flight, no longer as dust clouds but as airborne flowers. Butterflies flutter impetuously, appear to gather momentum, then dawdle a bit till they are almost motionless, and just when they seem a mere plaything of the wind, they begin to flutter again. Theirs is an erratic flight compared to that of birds, birds which suddenly flocked around us, as if sprung from the low line of hills. Most birds glide. They don't constantly flap their wings: like butterflies, their wingbeats are intermittent, and between times they spread their wings. But unlike butterflies, their flight effortlessly traces a harmonious arc. Hummingbirds are somewhere between birds and butterflies, in their bright colours, of course, but also in their ceaseless, electric flight. Maybe they're closer to insects. The air was a living mass of creatures and the buzzing of the bees and the flies and the barigüí and the mosquitoes was its breath. I began to breathe in time with them, I let myself be part of that low sound which at night swelled with the odd croaks of muddy creatures. We were nearly in the wetlands where water doubles happiness just as it doubles every image reflected in it, filling each one with plural lives.

So between mud and air we journeyed on, with me drunk on the scent of flowers and the Colonel's wine. Liz had decided the wagon was carrying too much so we set about lightening our load in a festive mood. The invisible threads connecting us were like hammocks, we swung to and fro singing in Spanish and English and in the language the three of us invented as we went along, in which Estreya played his part, trying to bark in harmony.

Most Were Naked and Beautiful

That's how they first glimpsed us, a procession led by a wagon carrying three people – a woman, a man and a two-spirit – singing in a strange language, and accompanied by a little black dog with amber eyes who barked along to the song, almost always in the right key; then came hundreds of cows marching and dancing along in quite a disorganised fashion but always managing somehow to keep the wagon in the middle, the youngest cows trotting happily onwards, butting one another occasionally; five beautiful horses free to gallop every which way only to come straight back to the cows and then run off again; six gentle oxen and some hens clucking in a cage at the back of the wagon. Above the cage was a gadget our observers didn't recognise and they feared was a weapon – though such a gay procession didn't tally with their idea of the army; they were already familiar with the stern discipline of soldiers, their dry cruelty, the humiliation born of hierarchy.

They followed us for a couple of days and we noticed straight away. Estreya barked at the trees, wagging his tail, incapable as my dog is of imagining humans offering anything other than shelter, food and play; Rosa noticed because he's a tracker and he knows about these things; Liz and I picked up on the Indians from Estreya and

Rosa's behaviour but we didn't allow ourselves to get spooked. We just kept on drinking the wine and singing, singing now to the eyes we thought we could make out in every tree; there were just three of us, we had to keep going, we could neither attack nor defend ourselves. We could only sing.

The desert – I had always believed that it was the land of the Indians, of the unseen people who were now watching us – was like a paradise. Or what I would call a paradise: the lagoons down yonder and the lagoons up over there were, curiously, higher up than some dry areas, and there were so many trees, in some places there was nothing but trees. The birds all sang at full screech: I don't know why birds screech nor am I sure that they really sing, the only animal I can safely say knows how to sing is my Estreya, but then what are the birds doing when they screech? They're calling out to other birds, showing their charms so they can make more birds. Life has a complex mechanism of self-perpetuation, cruel life employs beauty as a way to make us and to kill us, that's how it renews itself over and over again. The birds flew and it was a dance and it was also their way of finding food: thus the herons launched themselves into the water to swallow fish to keep themselves alive and to make more herons. Whether it was the wine, or the renewed freedom of having left the estancia, or both, I'd gone all contemplative. We hadn't caught up with our gauchos but we weren't alarmed because they were on horseback and had a huge advantage over us. They'd be leagues ahead until they stopped long enough for us to catch up. What we were nervous about was encountering the Indians.

We heard them first and then we smelt them. They were singing too and they were eating asado: that aroma guided us towards a plain between two mountains, to the banks of a sky-blue lagoon, a flowery meadow, and there they were, some armed and in soldiers' uniforms but ill-fitting ones, as if they had pulled their trousers over their heads and wore their hats over their private parts. Most were naked and beautiful: they were tall with broad shoulders and strong jaws, eyes shining as if continually lit by the power of the noonday sun, they had very dark shiny skin smeared with grease, and painted with white drawings like ghosts – they made the paint out of powdered bones – and wore headdresses made from flowers or feathers or a combination of the two, and seemed not to choose these adornments according to sex like we would do. They were gathered around fires in little groups, eating with knives and their fingers, when they smiled their teeth were as white as the paint that covered parts of their beautiful bodies, and there were so many of them; their tents were spread out all around, the tents also glistened from the same fat as they used on their skin and which was good for lots of things, like almost everything the Indians had. We had arrived on a sacred day when they were celebrating the bounties of summer, the summer that brought the beauty of flowers and animals and the generosity of the earth that gave forth its fruits, requiring no work beyond reaching a hand towards the trees, or snaring one of the many little creatures running around on the ground, or flashing a spear at the fish and the birds. That's how we saw them as we got near without knowing where to stop, no tent looked any more important than the rest. Perhaps we would stop at the first line of tents and then keep walking; we were just deciding what to do when they began to look at us and a group came forward. It was some of the naked ones who took the lead, not their warriors.

Time passed, probably just a twinkling, but it seemed longer due to a curious stillness, a stillness in which we all just looked; us at them and them at us, our cows at their cows, my dog at their dogs, the horses at everyone. Up until the naked people ahead of the other naked ones began to sing and walk forward: we did the same thing, singing as well, we walked with open arms, we did everything they did and we ended up merging with these Indians of pure splendour who smelled of fat and chañar trees in bloom and lavender, because that is what they put in the fat they used, so when I embraced Kaukalitrán I sank even deeper into the forest that is Indian Territory. Into the summertime I sank. Into the berries bursting red and replete from the bushes. Into the mushrooms growing in the shade of the trees. Into every single tree I sank. And I became aware of the whims of my heart, the different appetites my body could have: I wanted to be both the berry and the mouth biting into it.

I didn't have to wait long for my wish to be granted. The hug was followed by kisses, I felt Kaukalitrán pushing herself and her savage saliva into my mouth, she tasted of wild mint, ñandú leg, puma, ombú, the smoke of sweet daisies, caña and something bitter that I couldn't quite identify. 'Welcome to our celebration, my dear English girl-boy,' she said when we paused for breath. They spoke to us in perfect Spanish, they talked like Hernández because they'd learnt the language from their grand-parents who had learnt it on the estancia of Juan Manuel de Rosas, the Restorer of Laws who loved acting like royalty, and who had taken the eldest sons of the Indian chiefs hostage as a guarantee in a peace treaty. Or the ones he believed to be the chiefs, because the Selk'nam Nation changed chiefs continually and amicably, only occasionally causing squabbles that were resolved by the council of women elders or – if their advice was insuffi-cient – by the clean strike of a spear. Rosas had carried off the first-born of the peacemakers. Our Indians weren't

Selk'nam any more, they had mixed with the Tehuelche and quite a few Winkas, as they called the white man, but they had chosen to remember their most southerly forefathers. They told us that they were the desert and that they welcomed us with open arms. That they had been watching us approach for three days and that we should drink and eat and dance in their celebration of summer. Kaukalitrán said that to me, Catriel said it to Liz, and Millaray to Rosa. They said that looking into our eyes, never letting go of our hands, and that's how they led us to the lagoon they called Kutral-Có, the Water of Fire, and we would soon know why. The six of us sat on a tree trunk and they ate the golden cap of a thin-stemmed mushroom and offered some to us. We also ate bitter fruits. No one spoke for a while until Kaukalitrán made a gesture that seemed to take in the whole lagoon, the other two began laughing and the flamingos rose up into a single pink stain against the blue sky, revealing the water, which didn't know what colour to be amid all the commotion. The indecision of the water made me giggle, shyly at first, and then helplessly till I was in stitches: Kutral-Có doesn't know what colour to be, it's alive, the lagoon is an animal, look Estreya, I called my dog over, our sister the lake can't make her mind up! Look Kaukalitrán, look how my Estreya has the sun inside him! Look Liz, look what a beautiful puma Kaukalitrán is! Watch me run on my two ñandú feet, look how no one can catch me, Rosa, not even you with your lightning young horses. Look puma, see me outrun you! Come on Kauka, I want to swim. I took off my clothes and let myself be led by Kauka who knew the mud around her lagoon, Kutral-Có, where they celebrated summer every year, but I didn't feel any mud; I knew that I was stepping on the tongue of the animal I hadn't known was an animal, the bottom and the edges are the lagoon's tongue, the water is its body, and its body is full of stones and plants and fish and bits of tree. When Kauka and I got into its body we became fish, I turned silvery and slender like a surubí fish and like a surubí I grew a little beard which I smoothed against Kauka's body, which had become flat and wide and lead-grey like a pacú fish and I licked her golden pacú tummy while she floated in the water which had finally made its mind up; it was purple now with brownish scales around the brown of its tongue. I licked the golden tummy of my pacú fish that grew thinner and took on tiger stripes and, now a tararira fish, nibbled at me like I was a fish hook, she nibbled at me and just stayed there, hanging from me, my fish lady. I could see Liz on the tree trunk in the distance, her red hair aflame. She was naked too and they were painting her with brown paint; I saw her become a chestnut foal. Although I'd already seen her like that, I'd never seen her that way naked in the arms of another, nor had I seen myself naked in the middle of the body of a lagoon and in the arms of a tararira, and this new perspective made me laugh, Kauka laughed too, and we drifted apart as if our sexual embrace had dissolved in the water. We swam ashore. I wanted to be my real self too, I wanted my skin to be painted with the image that would lay me bare, I was a tigress tararira fish as well, or Kauka was. I decided I didn't care which and I lay down on the grass and let my body be painted by one of the machi, who had seen my tararira soul, and I saw Liz as a foal again and I kissed her on the back and Liz spoke to me in English saying tigress, my tigress, my mermaid, my girl, my good boy, my white gaucho girl, and my tigress again and we just collapsed in the mud with Kauka alongside us and with her Catriel and then Rosa and Millaray and we wallowed around until we were as frog-like as the frogs that were jumping around us and we mated as frogs there in the mud that seemed like the beginning of the world and just as it was in the beginning we all loved each other without shame and we didn't stop loving each other because the flamingos and that infinite pink returned, as though Wenumpau, the sky of the desert, took pleasure in showing us its luminous blood. That distracted us, it made us hungry and we ran back to the kutral, the fire, all of us brown and we had to hold back our ravenous hunger, we were only able to get our teeth into it after the ceremony, the cook divided up the ñandú on the fire into as many pieces as there were people. He didn't keep anything for himself or his assistant and Liz and Rosa and I held back so we could see how the Indians ate and we saw that they didn't rush, they told one another that there was roast meat and so the ones who had been given the biggest portions, the muscly breast of the ñandú, would grab a knife and cut off the best bit and give it back to the cook and his assistant, and only then did they let their crazed hunger take over and everyone gave in to gnawing like half-starved pumas. We lay down in the grass around the kutral, night was falling and with nightfall, of course, came the dew and we felt like rain-drenched earth and someone brought us some blankets made of feathers. Mine was pink and I fell asleep all flamingo, watching the sky bursting with stars and holding hands with Kauka and Liz, who was sucking all the milk from the Milky Way through the ring on her finger.

I woke a couple of hours later, by myself, and I didn't know what to wear: my gaucho clothes were ridiculous but they were the only ones I had so I went back to Kutral-Có and had a wash to get the mud off, as it was starting to itch, and I put them back on again and added my flamingo blanket as a poncho. By a kutral quite near to the big fire, the cooking fire — there were many fires, they made constellations on the ground with all those fires – were Liz and Rosa, dressed like the Indians, with white tunics made of heron feathers that had touches of gold and russet from the scales of pejerrey fish and capybara fur. They were all so beautiful, as exquisite as any animal, like all animals, like the animals from which the clothes had been made.

There was no centre, as I've said, nor any ruka that was bigger than the others, but bit by bit and surely because of the novelty we presented, the night became organised around our kutral. Rosa went to the wagon for the gifts we had brought. The Indians liked the mirrors and what could have seemed like childishness on their part turned out to make perfect sense to me: they looked at the beauty of their reflections and they were gorgeous, as were the old men and women with their furrowed skin wrinkled by sun and snow and their white hair; as were the women who had just given birth with their swollen breasts; as were the men dressed like soldiers; as were the women warriors, because amongst these Indians – my people, my nation – the tasks are divided according to the simple criteria of ability, desire, and need.

We also presented them with the barrel of caña and what was left of the wine and the black cockerels that had grown during the last storm. Kauka loved them and I imagined her feathered, dressed as a jet-black warrior. I'd seen her flex her bow next to a fire to warm the string, she was strong and black and flecked with light like the most luminous night. Once the kutral got going, the other foreigners also joined us. There were captive Englishwomen who walked around freely and came over to hear the news from Liz: the Queen's state of health, God save Her, how the railways were coming along, the power of the new machines, the slavery in the coal mines, the joy of the jewel-green fields of England, the force of the sea that alternated between lapping and lashing dear old Blighty. And they talked about this new life, they told Liz about freedom; she already knew a bit about that but she would find out a whole lot more and never want to go back to stiff upper lips, crossed legs nor even to England's green and pleasant land. There were also German scientists who went around collecting phosphorescent bones, as if trying to give substance to the devil's lantern, and who found fame by putting their names to dinosaur remains, much to the amusement of the Indians who cried with laughter every time someone showed them a skeleton called Roth or a lichen specimen – its delicate little leaves encased in a stone as transparent as Liz's ring – called Von Humboldt. There were exiles from the Republic of Argentina who were always too busy plotting to come over to us – the Indians put up with them but didn't like them, we don't like them because we knew that with them you never get more than brief alliances ripe with betrayal, different each time but nonetheless inevitable. And there were gauchos, hundreds of them, who were already dressed like the locals, including our gauchos, the ones we'd helped to escape from Hernández. And so many others. Among them there was a man who moved so delicately, his long braids swaying against his tunic of feathers as pink as mine and a sash around his waist. With the Indians, as I said, neither clothes nor way of living is determined by sex. He looked like a china disguised as a flamingo, you could just make out a touch of masculinity in his stubble, nothing else. He came over to me and suddenly I knew that what Hernández had said was true: it was Fierro, but now made more out of feathers than of Iron. I wanted to run away, but following behind him were my two little boys. Reader, I can't describe it, I just can't express the happiness that I felt in my body, the fullness in my soul, when I pressed my nose to their little heads and stayed there lost in the smell of my kids. They were beautiful and they hugged me so tight that I was forced to stay and listen to what Fierro had to say. Indians adore love stories and Fierro was in the habit of singing everything that had happened to him as well as plenty that hadn't, it was his way of earning his keep. Indians appreciate art as much as Hernández does, but they don't go around passing off gaucho verses as their own. Fierro would already have sung about us and Raúl to them, along with who knows what other verses. I let him come over and sit opposite me, guitar in hand, and we all listened to his verse.

Oh China, Love, Forgive Me Now

Oh China, love, forgive me now!
To God I've pleaded long
That he should bring us here as friends
So I to you could make amends
And ask your pardon for what offends
By singing you this song.

Your head of plaits you've shaven clean
On mine two plaits I braid;
The wood once hidden by the trees
Is now revealed, we see with ease
That when our loves we've failed to please
Our errors must be paid.

Josephine is now your name
A name that's sweet to hear,
I know that I have done you wrong
But if you'll listen to my song
You'll hear how I have suffered long
And you'll be kind, my dear.

'Twas I who killed your love Raúl
'Twas I who took his life,
A strong man he, a fair one too,

Whose face was honest, whose heart was true,
But all his strength I did undo
With the blade of my gaucho knife.

Raúl abandoned me for you,
Like a rancher's bastard child,
As cattle leave their dung behind
And ñandús sprint off unconfined
So he left me – t'wards you inclined
And – jealous – I ran wild.

You I won at cards one night
By filling El Negro with drink.
He lost the game, he lost his life
That Negro runt was born for strife
I can't say I've never flashed a knife
But I've since had time to think.

As you stole my Raúl from me,
I stole you from his side,
You thought sore pride had caused my wrong
But 'twas fear of gossip that spurred me on
Lest folk found out my heart he'd won
And us they should deride.

But after that my conscience pricked
I wanted to play fair
With home and wife, with children too
And all of that was thanks to you
But the Colonel came, and so, adieu!
Conscription was my share.

Army life was rough and hard,
An estancia we had to build,
Ploughing here and fencing there

A moment's rest was very rare
No chance of sneaking in caña there
Or they'd stake you out to be grilled!

Scores of lashes, little bread
No wages on the cards.
The foreman kept them stashed away
He'd rather not give us our pay
Instead he bought some meat each day
For the chimangos who were his guards.

China, I was lean and sore
That life of a dog was grim,
'Progress', said he, 'we shan't obstruct
And Argentina we'll construct!'
Forget all that! We're damn well fucked
Building an estancia for him.

So sad and worn was I, my love
That I sat me down to sing
My old guitar was still my friend
Its strings still with my voice did blend
To the tired men my songs I'd lend
Round the campfire in a ring.

So things weren't quite so bad with me;
The thousand gaucho men –
Who conscripts were – admired my song,
But though its words to me belong
That thief Hernández did me wrong
By taking up his pen.

He made a book from songs of mine
And signed it with his name:
My words he changed – as if I'd say

'Become the judge's friend this day!'
A judge your warmth will ne'er repay
He plays the Colonel's game.

I flew to the Colonel in a rage
My verses to defend:
'You scoundrel! You stole my songs!' I said.
They staked me out, I wasn't fed
For three whole days – near left for dead –
And that was not the end.

He came and asked me straight to say
If it was my belief
That all those songs were mine alone;
I swore they were, and did bemoan
Hernández calling them his own
The swindling, song-grabbing thief!

Well then they whipped and flayed me sore
Till my back was raw and red:
My blood flowed out as once my song
Had flowed like springs, so sweet and strong,
The Colonel wished me dead ere long
And on the ground I bled.

But as I lay a-dying there
One night came Cruz to me,
A haloed light shone round his head
My bonds he cut, as one we fled
And as the rays of dawn were shed
We rode together, free.

In a hovel rough we hid,
Our bed the horses shared
So no one would our hide-out spy.

At night Cruz hunted, by and by
The kill he'd cook, his food I'd try
For me like a mother he cared.

He fed me cuy, vizcacha, rat,
He made me soup from bones,
Ñandú eggs, leaves of ombú,
Wild fox and beef he'd stew,
Chimango flesh he had me chew
Cooked over heated stones.

Like Jesus rising from the tomb
In two days I was well:
The third day dawned, he kissed my lips
His salt-sweet mouth mine did eclipse
He mounted me, he held my hips
To heaven I came from hell.

The sun shone on my arse that hour.
My spurs I cast away,
A moment more I couldn't wait
To suck him dry and with him sate
My lust for him, then lie prostrate;
Such freedom I knew that day.

To you in words I can't explain
The pleasure that I felt
To have his prick come into me
In paradise I seemed to be
Through flesh was God revealed to me
And at his feet I knelt.

I thanked him that I had been born
Such pleasure to partake,
To be beloved so well as this

To be pinned down with utter bliss
Sweet Jesus, what a marvel 'tis —
What fools those straight men make!

When we two came upon this place
We made ourselves a tent
As others do, with cattle skin,
With space to do our cooking in
And I was here with Cruz my dear
And we were well content.

But little did it please our God
Our livelihood to bless:
The smallpox came upon us all
Our friends around us ill did fall
'Gainst fate I railed. Cruz's dying call
Destroyed my happiness.

Thus kneeling at his deathbed cold
To God I Cruz commend.
The light went hither from my eyes
I fainted then, as if the skies
A bolt had sent to cease my cries
At seeing his life end.

So, China, now you understand
How in my life I've paid
For wrongs I did you years ago,
I've paid in full, and you should know
That for our children I did go
And with me they have stayed.

Will you forgive me, Josephine?

The Indians had pressed close around us and were very persuasive: they made us reach out and embrace each other a while. When I said yes, I would forgive him, they whooped and began belting out those high-pitched songs, with wailing choruses to different tunes that were all their own. It took me a while to understand their music. From shouting they moved to dancing. We danced, and it was from the peak of one of my flamenco leaps, frolicking like a tararira fish, that I saw Liz kissing a gringo who had to be none other than Oscar. I didn't have time to feel sorry for myself because Kauka led me back to the lake where I plunged in once again and learnt to swim underwater, breathing through a hollow reed in my mouth. I learnt to get in a canoe, paddle, and then moor it among the reeds, letting the wind rock us gently like little girls. I learnt to see the dawn from inside, that's the view from a canoe in Kutral-Có. I slept with Kauka, in her ruka, in an animal-skin hammock that swung to the rhythm of her body and mine, everything rocked me gently in her arms. The Indians are creatures of Mewlen, the wind. That first night in the tent I learnt to fly, I started becoming Indian, writhing against Kauka's body on the deep pink, almost red, feathers, letting her warrior fingers touch me inside as they did her bow and arrows, she is strong and beautiful and I want her beside me, and I soon became one of her tribe, almost as quickly as I had become one of the family with Liz, Estreya and Rosa; there amongst the Indians my family grew with my own sons, Juan and Martín, with Kauka and her daughters, Nahuela and Kauka, who are also my daughters now, and — most unlikely of all — with Fierro and Oscar. Our families are large, linked by more than bloodlines. This is my family now.

We also learnt to belong to Mewlen, to build our rukas so that they provide us with shelter and rest without being cumbersome, and can be taken down and put up again without much trouble whenever we need to. We learnt to ask forgiveness of the lambs we slaughtered, promising that no part of them would be sacrificed in vain, and drinking their blood still warm, while holding them tight and speaking slowly in their ears – poor little things – so that they should die loved. We learnt to sing in choruses that to the uninitiated seem like shouting but which take months to learn. And we learnt to swim in the lake and make clothes out of feathers and shoot with a bow and arrow.

I woke up in Kauka's ruka and she offered me a corncob and peppermint tea, laughing at me with smiling eyes as she gave me my breakfast and kissed me. Her daughters came along and the four of us all ate together. Afterwards, when we were onto our second cob, one of the girls' fathers arrived and he joined us for the rest of breakfast before taking the girls off to teach them to paddle and fish from the canoe. The fine art of spear fishing is something that my two have picked up as if they had always done it, skilful as diving birds since they were five or six years old. Kauka had to go, she was on sentry duty: we the Iñchiñ people, a name we gave ourselves, take turns doing jobs. I watched her set off, in the rag-tag army clothes, shining bronze and riding bareback on her white mare.

I started walking between the rukas looking for Fierro's and I found it. The inside was all hung with feathers, my two boys and all his other children were fast asleep in hammocks that looked like wings. The kids were like little chicks in Fierro's tent, and he was sleeping on a kind of cloud, a white feather mattress, dressed in a tunic of the same colour. I stood there looking at him like a dumb animal, lost for words; I'd never imagined I would see the beast looking so angelic. I had breakfast again with all his family, which is also mine now, with all the children of this person who'd once been my husband and was now a loving mother to a whole string of little ones. He asked my forgiveness again and told me the whole story, his great love for Cruz, and his deep sadness at the death of that most beautiful warrior: our lives will always be intertwined, Josefina. He told me about all the new things he'd learnt to do: the Colonel's gymnastics that he still did every morning because that really was a good thing, Jo, like learning to read and write, the clothes he was designing out of all different coloured feathers ready for next summer, rainbow dresses, China, can you imagine? And how much he wanted to look after all the Iñchiñ children, he didn't see any reason why he couldn't. They sat happily on his lap, pulled his braids, said I want chocolate Mama, played with his guitar, let the dogs into the tent. Estreya was beside himself, he was smiling so much his mouth reached his ears, even though the kids were pulling his tail and climbing onto him as if he were a horse. I said to Fierro I've got to go. You're off to see the English woman, but you don't fool me, you're sleeping with Kauka too. Take the two boys, they'll help you out. So I went off to my wagon, the one that had been mine, along with my boys and with the dog, as I was scared to go alone; I found Liz and Oscar holding hands and drinking tea, happily reunited. This is Josephine, Liz introduced me to Oscar, and he stood up and embraced me, thanking me warmly for taking care of his beloved wife. He motioned for me to sit down and gave me a cup of tea. The kids clung to my legs and Estreya couldn't stop wagging his tail, he was so happy at being with us, a full Iñchiñ too from that day onwards. Rosa, who was no fool, turned up as well and joined in the tea ceremony. And Oscar told us part of his story: he'd met Hernández too. He'd gone to a neighbouring estancia, not to Hernández's fort, but the Colonel had been to visit, as he always loved speaking English and didn't get much chance to do so out in the pampas, so Oscar listened to him and gave him a whisky to make him feel at home. Oscar really did listen, and Hernández invited him to come and work with him as foreman on his estancia. Hernández talked to him about rural industry, progress in the pampas, the railways that 'you and your fellow Britons' would bring to the furthest corners of Argentina. He talked about the concert of nations, an end to world hunger which would begin here, right there where the two of them were sitting, he emphasised this to Oscar, stamping his foot, and Oscar looked confused; since arriving in the country he'd seen nothing but emaciated gauchos with swollen bellies and their ribs sticking out. He also told Oscar that his English employer had been deceived: the land marked on his map was still in Indian Territory. It wouldn't be easy trying to set up an estancia there, and anyway it wouldn't be good for anything but rearing goats, the Colonel said, snorting with laughter. However, he also said, Oscar was a free man, could do what he liked, the Argentine Nation wasn't going to hold one of the Queen's subjects hostage. He himself was heading back to his own estancia at dawn and Oscar could go with him or do as he pleased. They embraced like brothers and agreed they'd set off together the next day. But when Oscar approached the Colonel's carriage the following morning, he saw him there snoring away, and had to shout to wake him up. The old man looked at him, and not remembering either him or their conversation nor, most probably, anything of what had gone on the previous night, rewarded him with a day of staking out for having rudely awoken him. Oscar knew then that he had to escape and he began to make preparations. He gave himself a week to recover from the hangover and the spread-eagling, to stash away a couple of shotguns and some beef jerky and plan his getaway: then he cut through the fence that kept the horses in and made as if to go after them with the gauchos. He managed to heave himself bareback onto one, lassoed two others and off he went, thus stealing three horses from the Argentine National Army. Of course he wasn't the only one to take advantage of the situation, but he reckoned he was conspicuous as the only gringo deserter, so he headed off into Indian Territory. And he was sure that Liz – he called her Liz too – would manage to make her way there; she's not only beautiful but bright and brave, he said, kissing her again. She took my hands, and became a bit tearful. I'd found my sons, she said, she knew how much I'd missed them, she continued. She was lying, I'd hardly spoken a word about them to her; I think she was looking for an excuse to touch me while she looked at me, without having to hide her emotion in front of Oscar. I'll give you back the ring that belonged to your grandmother, she lied again, and she grasped my hand, taking my finger – that had given her so much pleasure – and stroked it while sliding the ring on and I felt as though the brilliance of the galaxy went straight from the vastness of space into my heart. She kissed me on the lips and it was almost like when I got married, all that was missing was the priest's blessing, though there was something of a blessing from Oscar, who kissed me too saying that his family was my family, and mine was his, and he began joking with my children in English, they already knew one another and could understand him perfectly. 'Everything's turned out so nicely,' said Rosa, and I heard a collective sigh: at that point I realised that several Indians had been hiding and watching the scene, as if they knew about us. Did they know? Indians absolutely adore love stories; that same night, Liz started reading them a translation of *Romeo and Juliet* and they wouldn't let her go to bed until she'd finished it. It was quite a sight, seeing those uncommonly brave and heroic warriors crying for hours over the lovers' death.

That same day there was another ceremony with mushrooms and I slept with other women. And with several Iñchiñ men sheathed with lamb-intestine coverings: no part of the animal was wasted and anyway, if they didn't, we'd end up with so many children we wouldn't be able to feed them all. I managed to find my way back to Kauka's tent while still in the form of a puma: I went in on all fours, growling, and there I stayed, roaring in the hammock until all the feathers flew off it, they whirled upwards and – when my body couldn't bear any more bliss – I watched them float slowly down. The summer celebrations last for four months, it was now the last month and every day I experienced Iñchiñ life in all its glory. I'd already become air in the desert, as if preparing me for becoming Iñchiñ, then I'd thought I was becoming English, but no: England isn't airy, or light; it's the bowels of the earth, the place where iron is found and which spurs the planet's onward motion. Among my Iñchiñ people I also became water because although we Iñchiñ are firstly wind, with that summer feast we started becoming river, threatened by Winka outsiders. We knew about the government of Argentina's plans from what the Colonel had told us, and our brothers and sisters knew from the newspapers they got hold of every time they went to villages to exchange their feathers and hides for tobacco, caña, or little mirrors or whatever they fancied. Kauka, for example, has a writing desk and a chair in her ruka: she sits there to write her poems and letters negotiating on behalf of the Iñchiñ people. Through the exchange of letters and messengers, and remembering what the Colonel had told us and what we'd seen in the newspapers, we were sure that the government offensive was going to be one of fire and fury. The ground would run with blood.

But We Don't Have Any Weapons

We were on the move by autumn. My people have very small carts that can be pulled quickly by a single horse, my people travel like the wind, nimble and light; we don't want to crush anything underfoot.

Every night, once the ground was studded with the stars of our campfires, we would discuss what to do. We could confront the Winka, the white man; courage wasn't in short supply. Nor indeed were white people who knew how to wage war like Winkas. But we don't have any weapons, pointed out Oscar and Liz and all the foreigners, much to the dismay of the Indian warriors and dissident Argentines, and to the delight of the old men and women who know what life is worth, because life starts to be worth more as death draws near. A decision gradually emerged: people of water we would become and take ourselves off to the green gold of the islands, to Y pa'û, which is to the North and to the East, where summers are very long and the kuarahy, the sun, shines bright but reaches the earth restless and broken by shadows, draped in leaves, almost a plant itself. The pira leap like lightning in the gentle ripples of the Paraná River, and hundreds of little channels, ysyry, come and go from its winding course, birds never leave, the ype swim with their little ducklings in a row, the guasutí deer have big hooves but are tame because hardly anyone ever hunts them, and the kapi'ybaras work ceaselessly with their little paws. We paddle around on the river and all year long we organise races and competitions for fun and to make us strong, both young and old, men and women, and two-spirits. Y pa'û lands are rich but hard to cultivate and Argentines are lazy: we counted on them leaving us more or less in peace until they discovered what could be grown easily in the marshland. We the Iñchiñ became a water-going people and we learnt to live alongside the Guaraní people on the river banks; Rosa's sapukái made him a good ambassador, and they also loved our mushrooms and our celebrations. They call Rosa vy'aty, the happy one, and we're starting to call him that as well. They call us Ñande.

Now the sound of the water, the undertow and the tides are our music, and they watch over us. Our rivers are alive and the streams are animals, they know that we live as one, that we only kill what we need to eat and that our fine native bulls and our healthy cows are our livelihood; all we ask of the beasts is that they wander freely on the islands and that they eat and shit, they are Iñchiñ too. What little work we have is done contentedly, though not without effort: we build wampos to put our cows on when the water starts to rise; when there are floods they float peacefully, tied to the branches of the yvyra. You should see the cows up there when the water subsides all of a sudden and some of them get trapped like brown fruit among the willow leaves, watching us a bit startled with their ever-gentle eyes. No doubt they're amazed by that aerial view of the world, a perspective they never quite get used to and which has them protesting quietly, perhaps fearing that mooing too loudly might send them tumbling to the ground. Getting them down from the treetops without hurting them is a task we are now experts at, we do it so deftly and smoothly that the cattle look like flags being lowered; as they come down swaying gently, the air is filled with their perplexed lowing.

We grow pumpkins and muskmelon, potatoes and watermelon. Other plants too, plants not for eating with our occasional plates of guasutí meat or beef or pira, but rather to help us to think. Or to be strong. Or to laugh. We grow them on wampos piled with earth and tied to the trees.

Light is Doubled on the Islands

The land gets muddier and muddier until it gives way to the croaks and cheeps of a reed bed, the air on the banks sings with the criss-crossing of guyrá in flight, riverbanks are a little luxury the pampa allows itself, the cows bathe with a little persuasion, slipping and slithering; the land then re-emerges from beneath the river, and although it must be the same land, it's now full of trees, their naked roots at the water's edge. We put our rukas up a little way back from the shore; rivers in the pampa can suddenly swell with silent but ferocious energy, and you wake up submerged if you don't know the sounds and ways of the impulsively rising and falling ysyry.

When we reached the far shore, there where the pampa drowns, some of us swam across the river, the ones who'd chosen the southernmost peoples as their ancestors, and who would quickly remember how to canoe. They swam across naked and those of us left on terra firma had a contest hurling axes at the trees which we then, in sorrow, had to pull down, giving thanks for their life which we'd taken in order to make rafts. In this way we gradually became people of water, and people of wood. Oscar was among those who swam across: his sort knew about canoes, but knew nothing about the rafts of the Selk'nam peoples. They soon got the idea,

Oh, wampos, they said, and made rafts – so much better than ours, darling, Oscar enthused to Liz. Those were our first wampos, we used them to get the oxen across, just a few good strong ones that would then pull the next few wampos – you really have to pull hard when your hooves are sinking into the mud – beautiful oxen, our dear mansún, the ones that carried across everything we had. As they made the wampos, they became more skilled and started making wampo-rukas: we live in floating houses and moor them with strong leather ropes that can withstand any flood, so we go up whenever the river rises and as it subsides, we go down with it. Sometimes it sinks so low that we end up almost stuck in the mud, rich pickings for the mosquitoes, or rather we would be if Liz hadn't gone to the village to buy nets. She went dressed in her English clothes, gave no explanation, and simply showed them a piece of mesh and asked to buy up all they had left. The Argentines must have wondered what on earth the gringa was up to; when they pressed her she said in the worst Spanish that she could muster, wedding dresses, bride, gown, and they seemed satisfied with that, imagining a throng of gringas disembarking to come and inter-marry and improve the stock. So some days we wake beached in mud and other days perched atop the yvyra, and where once there were islands there's nothing but river everywhere. The Paraná is an animal that likes to live in segments, just as our bodies have limbs, but then feels the urge to reconnect and to overflow its banks as if there were something beyond itself, as if the islands weren't part of its body, though they are. When the river remembers this we wake to find ourselves and our rukas up in the trees, with our canoes butting up against the rukas and treetrunks dragged along by the current banging against us or piling up in dykes on either side. Other times we wake to find the Paraná's smooth back has become a garden, we fall asleep in the moon-thrummed dark and awake surrounded by aguapé looking like green cabbages with bright purple flowers which stand out against that green matched only by distant English wheat fields in spring, though richer yet: a beautiful, vivid green of a thousand hues, so many shades that a single word can't contain them all and new words become necessary. We use Guaraní words: aky for the tender green of young shoots, hovy for the deep blue-green of all the leaves at dusk, hovyu for the intense shade everything takes on in summer, and we are still pondering what to call the dry colour of the reeds even though they are always damp, what to call the silvery underside of willow leaves, what to call the little islets and aguapé that are dotted all over the back of the Paraná and its ysyry, what to call the dark green grass that grows in the shade of the trees, what to call the ita poty which grows on damp stones, what to call the plants like green plates with tiny floats on their stems and roots, tough discs that can hide snakes and pumas. They too travel downstream whether they like it or not, the Paraná drags them along when it rushes down from the northern land, the Guaraní land, that belongs to us too a little ever since they began calling us Ñande as well as Iñchiñ. That north that we are soon going to explore once we have negotiated with the Guaraní, the negotiations are long discussions that end up in new relationships, in a larger sense of Us. We will do it on our wampos, just a few of us, and using the ysyry: you can't go against the Paraná, it's a great and powerful river, and no one travels on it against its wishes. You have to follow the current, go where it leads. So we will take a different path, head back up the channels we came down; the ysyry are less powerful and, as luck would have it, too narrow for the navy's gunboats to navigate. We can't declare ñorairo and fight until we're ready. And we don't have any weapons.

Contemplating the Trees

Nobody works every day on the Y pa'û islands: we take turns, working one month in three. When it's our turn, we make sure our cows don't sink into the tuju and if they do start to sink everyone helps out: we keep watch so the floods don't take us by surprise. It all takes time, corralling the cows onto the wampos, putting out grass and water for them, calming them down so that they stand still enough to keep their balance, getting up there with them and patting them so that their breath is as slow and even as though they were in a meadow full of tender shoots of grass. Our plants are also up on wampos: these ones are enormous rafts with walls along the sides to keep everything in and they're full of earth, not so much that they can't float, but just enough for the roots of the plants to spread. For those of us not working the day goes by contemplating the trees, we never get tired of lying on the ground watching the play of light and shadow between the waving branches, their edges are bathed in a splendour which in Great Britain – Liz isn't really British anymore but she can still remember – you only see in the haloes around saints' heads in churches. Our leaves – those of our yvyra, our whole jungle – give off an aura of wondrous vegetable sanctity.

If we wake up early we greet the dawn from inside a

cloud, one that descends from the sky and rises from the rivers and streams in the early hours, the Paraná's tatatina: a cloud that prevents us from seeing anything except its insides which are luminous and opaque at the same time. An impossible cloud; how can something luminous be opaque? London lives in a cloud like that for a good part of the year, but its cloud is pinkish from all the smoke from the engines of the machines and ours is white like a bone from Our Lord God. The tatatina imposes a kind of peace: we just boil water to make mate and tea or grill some corn for the children, our mitã, they usually know who their parents are but they live with everyone, we all look after them and they come and go from ruka to ruka even though they keep their things in one hut in particular. We do the same. I share one with Kauka, but I can sleep and wake up in any other, wherever I am when I get drowsy and succumb to sleep; if not next to my warrior lady it might be beside Liz, who welcomes me of an evening for her curries and her stories, and some nights into her bed too. Sometimes I stay with Rosa who teaches the mitã the knack of breaking in horses, and sometimes I stay at Fierro's with his children and mine, where both of us have taken to writing. I sleep with my loves, I leave with Estreya after listening to songs, after playing games, after smoking or drinking the herbs we grow, that's a year-round undertaking, testing their flavour and their effects at the same time as mixing and grafting them together to create new plants.

As a result, we have an angel's trumpet that tastes of narã orange and berry, its fruit grow like weeds in Y pa'û; a tea that first blinds you, then takes you deep into your soul, a tea that transports you to the centre of the divine light and from there allows you to see that the whole world is a single animal, us and the ypyra leaves and the surubí catfish and the chajá screamer bird, and the giraffes

and the praying mantis mamboretá and the passion
flower mburucuyá, and the jaguar and the dragons
and the micuré possum, and the camuatí bee, and the
mountains and the elephants and the Paraná and even
the British railways and the huge swathes of land cleared
by the Argentines. We also have a herb that you smoke
that tastes of itself, of its own sweet and rough flower, and
also of warm bread and cheese rolls and marmalade made
from lemon and narã, the bitter orange from the deltas, a
happy herb called vy'aty that takes away pain and fills our
eyes with warmth, that makes the world more friendly
and other people companions we can laugh with. We
have mushrooms that we've been enriching with flavours
to make them less bitter: quince, tararira, different types
of water hyacinth, fresh wild lettuce, pure Paraná river
water, merõ melons and curry. Mushrooms are important
to us, they're for eating during ceremonies, never alone,
because mushrooms are are gifts to us from the very belly
of the earth, and life and death are in that tyeguy, all
mixed up together, one producing the other. Mushrooms
can make gods appear, it can happen that you stretch out
your body and then find you can't see your feet let alone
touch them, it can happen that the thing that normally
separates you from everyone else vanishes, it can happen
that the devil sticks out his tail and you fall into hell. You
emerge changed from mushrooms, the same but different,
mushrooms give people divine perspectives and these
perspectives from beyond life and death can be terrifying.
Or liberating. You need to have a machi wise woman
nearby when you take mushrooms. We have special rukas
and wampos for eating them, we have machis ready to
guide the journeys of visitors who are new to all this.
We also have a plant that we don't really like but that we
cultivate because we need it: we chew its leaves during
hard times, when floods or wars mean we have to work

all day and all night. These are the times when we need women and men to lead us: we always have a few chiefs, they take it in turns and don't usually have to do anything, but in times of crisis they're in charge and you have to put up with that until it's all over. Kauka's one of them, she leads a group along with an Englishman called Air, who spends his time fishing without much success and reciting limericks. In my nation, women have the same power as men. We don't care about the vote because we all vote and because we can have as many chieftesses as chieftains and we can also have two-spirits in charge. Even Fierro, who here on the islands has become a she and taken the name Kurusu – which is a woman's or kuña's name in Guaraní and a homage to the person who made her female, that's right, Cruz – even Kurusu Fierro has been a chieftess in periods of war with the Guaranís. That was in the beginning when they didn't want to accept us as neighbours, and when they hadn't yet come to any of our vy'aty ceremonies or tried our mushrooms, which they call marangatú. Even I, who can be woman and man, have had to lead the charge during a terrible flood and a skirmish with the Argentines, who feared we wouldn't let them transport their grain and hides down our Paraná. Kauka, who is one of our bravest and wisest warriors, has led terrible battles, the kind that fill the ysyry with bodies that the water then hurries to carry out to sea, wanting those to be pearls that were their eyes.

Otherwise, our time is our own apart from that one month in each season when it's our turn to work. During the other two we have fun competing at tree climbing, spearing leaping dorado fish, making dolls and gods with braided reeds, telling stories and singing songs about love and war, and rowing. Liz, Rosa and I are the fastest: travelling these waterways together is something we really love, the three of us, our canoes strapped together, rowing through its ysyry travelling as one, and we win all the weighted wampo races in Y pa' û. We train nearly every morning when we don't have to work, provided it's not raining too much, but even sometimes in torrential rain, when we compete in wet laden wampos. We're unbeaten and that's why we're the ones who carry the animals and plants when we migrate: the three of us bringing up the rear, each in our own kayak, the rukas on a small wampo at night, Rosa calming the cows and the dear oxen who no longer have to carry anything and can enjoy the same unencumbered life as the rest of us, they are Iñchiñ too. Oscar and Kauka lead the way, they command the flotilla of kayaks covered in branches that are at the vanguard of our migration, those that go ahead, making sure no nasty surprises lie in store. We make our way slowly, waiting for favourable currents, lingering on the islands where we find fruit trees, or where dorados and other pira jump enthusiastically in the rippling streams, or when we see bees hovering in the air. We meet up with our other loves, we sleep with them on those calm nights. During storms the three of us with Estreya tether ourselves to the strongest tree trunks, and caress the animals to reassure them as we steady ourselves against the currents.

I Wish You Could See Us

I wish you could see us, see our little steamboat, our wampos carrying cattle, rukas, horses, healing plants, our canoes and kayaks alongside, our nation slowly migrating along the channels of the Paraná: a whole people silently advancing along the limpid ysyry, which breathe the peace of flood and ebb, of whiskered fish and clinging tuju of the riverbed; our rivers that can hide and reveal the yvyra roots around their islands; our rivers full of flowers that float on the surface while catfish poke around in the murky silt beneath; our rivers of leaping pira, dorados thrusting their powerful bodies out of the water as if the river's insides were bursting open with sunlight. I wish you could see us, we the Iñchiñ people, now Ñande, silently migrating, rowing with love because only with love can we dip and pull our oars through the body of the Paraná. I wish you could see us with our feathered rukas billowing in the wind, quietly and calmly we go, each person's skin painted with their animal self, all heading north. I wish you could see us; but no one will. We migrate in autumn along rivers unnavigable by Argentine and Uruguayan boats. We migrate to escape the cold, we migrate so that we're never where they expect us to be. We migrate when the tatatina, the Paraná's voracious mist, swallows everything up, when

dawn is white blindness and things can only be distin-
guished by their sound, if they make any sound: low tones
of water lapping against the islands; the rhythmic sound
of oars dipping in the river; high-pitched screeching and
trilling of birdsong and the barking from near and far of
all the dogs on our island and on the neighbouring or
outlying islands. The tatatina signals the onset of autumn,
time for us to make tracks, and we are ready in a matter
of days; in less than a week we're all on our wampos
covered with branches and with clumps of reeds along
the edges; we imitate part of the landscape, part of the
Paraná riverbank and we are swallowed up into the cloud
blanketing land and river. The canoes go first, and are lost
at once in the mist, then the rukas with our people and
children, behind them our plants and lastly the animals. I
wish you could see us; but no one will. We know how to
leave as if vanishing into thin air: imagine a people that
disappears, a people whose colours, houses, dogs, clothes,
cows and horses all gradually dissolve like a spectre: their
outline turns blurry and insubstantial, the colours fade,
and everything melts into the white cloud. And so we go.

TRANSLATORS' NOTE

The *Adventures of China Iron* is a kaleidoscopic book. Twist the lens, let the pieces settle and each time you see a different perspective.

We saw a novel that dialogues playfully with nineteenth-century Argentinian history, notionally set in 1872, the year that José Hernández's epic poem *Martín Fierro* was published. As a highly provocative spin-off from this classic which narrates the trials and tribulations of an outlaw gaucho, the novel finds its feisty heroine in the shape of Fierro's young wife, here named China Iron. Whereas in the original poem she is relegated to a few lines, in Gabriela Cabezón Cámara's novel she takes centre stage, along with her Scottish fellow-traveller Liz.

Her travels through Argentina call to mind the many existing nineteenth-century travel narratives of British travellers in Argentina, with their eyes on imperial expansion (such as George Chaworth Musters' *At Home with the Patagonians* or Florence Dixie's *Across Patagonia*). They also powerfully and unsentimentally evoke the vanishing life of the gauchos (encapsulated in Ricardo Güiraldes' *Shadows on the Pampas*), the estancias with their cattle lore, rural poverty and hardship, and the unpleasant realities of conscription.

Turn the kaleidoscope, and the focus shifts to the world of nineteenth-century scientists and naturalists. We feel the presence of Alexander von Humboldt and his awe of the landscape, Charles Darwin's marvelling at the variety of species (the ñandú known also as Darwin's rhea streaks across the novel), and William Henry Hudson's nostalgic narratives for rural Argentina such as *Far Away and Long Ago* or *The Ombú*. Turn it again and we have a send-up of all this – a playful pastiche, queering Argentina's national myth of the noble virile gaucho.

Perhaps the most rewarding view through the kaleidoscope, however, is that of China's own story, a narrative of boundless curiosity and discovery. The breathlessly eager China takes us through her sexual re-awakening, her growing awareness of the beauties of her native land, and the broadening of her linguistic horizons, from imperial concepts to indigenous colours, from British English to Guaraní.

All these different views in the kaleidoscope presented us with challenges. Firstly, the poetry: the novel quotes some stanzas verbatim from Hernández's original *Martín Fierro* poem, and also devotes one whole chapter to a re-writing of a key scene, maintaining the original poetic form and metre, but radically altering the content. We chose not to use the existing 1935 translation into English by Walter Owen, but to re-translate the original as well as the additional verses, in the spirit of reinterpreting Fierro for a different context, whilst preserving the pace and drama.

Secondly, there is the challenge of the wide vocabulary used for flora, fauna and geographical features, much of which is unique to Argentina or to the Southern Cone of South America. This is frequently overlaid with political, social and historical elements which together produce words and concepts that are rich and dense with allusions, connotations and cultural specificity. 'China' posed a particular problem, since the word variously means girl, woman, wife or servant, carrying strong racial and class connotations, yet it is also (when capitalised) the name of the heroine herself, despite it not really being an individual name. Also problematic were the adjectives British, English and Scottish, which are used almost interchangeably in the original; from this side of the pond, these are clearly distinct identities, but not so from the Argentinian perspective.

The introduction of Guaraní vocabulary in the third part of the novel produces a deliberate foreignising effect on the Spanish-speaking reader of the original text, since the words will be unfamiliar to most readers of Spanish. Their appearance increasingly immerses the reader in the indigenous community into which China and her fellow travellers become accepted. The physical journey charted in the novel is thus paralleled by a linguistic journey into new territory. As translators, we consciously maintained this deliberate foreignisation, preserving that sense of going beyond one's own linguistic comfort zone and embracing new ways of conceptualising and naming the world.

Stylistically, the novel is complex; not only does it allude to all the above-mentioned discourses, but it does so in a voice which combines China's initial naivety and wonder with her later experience and new-found knowledge. The narrative is exuberant, with many long sentences punctuated only by endless commas; making such structures sound convincing in English is challenging. The dry humour which touches upon the history of Argentinian-British relations is essential to the spirit of the novel, but needs to be worn lightly. Liz, in explaining Britain to young China, says that 'The land ends abruptly there, as if England had been cut off from the rest of the world with an axe, as if the land had been forcibly condemned to an insularity which those of us who live there, we, the British, darling, try to overcome by dint of force.' What would Liz make of our attempt to overcome insularity by dint of translation?

We are grateful to the spry talent of our editor Fionn Petch at Charco Press, to Carolina Orloff, and for the support of the School of Literatures, Languages and Cultures at the University of Edinburgh.